Asheville Hearts

Mary L. Ball

ALL RIGHTS RESERVED

Publishers Note:
This is a work of fiction. All names, characters, places, and events are the work of the author's imagination. Any resemblance to real persons, places, or events is coincidental.

All Bible references used are from the New International Version of the Bible.

Asheville Hearts   Mary L. Ball

"And now these three remain: faith, hope and love. But the greatest of these is love."
~ 1 Corinthians 13:13

One

*B*arbary hustled up the stairs and launched every other step. At twenty-five, there were times when she still acted like a teenager.

She strolled down the massive hallway of her childhood home, to the west wing and knocked on Grandfather's door.

"Come in." He maneuvered his wheelchair and hit pause on the audio player.

"How are you today?" Barbary kissed his cheek, took a seat on the antique settee, and ran her hand over the faded material. Grandfather insisted on keeping the discolored furniture to remind him of her grandmother.

"I'm fine, listening to my new novel, *Wall of Time*. The author paints a wonderful picture of Western North Carolina."

"You're always engrossed in books about the region." She smiled and glanced at his thinning, gray hair.

"Some areas of the world are special to me." The mountains here are nice, still, there's something to be said about those southern hills. I especially like Bellmore Gardens. One of my favorites out of all the places I've been."

"Why?" Barbary noted his once sturdy body, now bent and lanky.

"The scenery there is wonderful. Built back in the eighteenth century, the owner passed the gardens down through the family. In the nineteen hundreds they turned the place into a public attraction with an inn, winery, and many gardens to explore. The people there were pleasant, too. *Ashevillians* is

9

what they call themselves." He smiled. "If memory serves, I stayed in the area for six months before I continued my travels. A year later, I came to New Mexico. Your grandmother relocated here from California." His chuckle cracked. "The first day I met her, your smart, beautiful grandmother stole my heart.

"After your grandmother passed away, I toyed with the idea of going back to Asheville."

"Grandfather, why didn't you?"

"Surgery slowed me down." He touched his back. "I never healed properly. Now, I'm older and can't get around. If we didn't have an elevator, I probably wouldn't even be able to go downstairs."

"You have a lot of years left." She grinned, attempting to lift his spirits and silently hoped her words were true.

"I've outlived your grandmother and your lovely mother." He sipped his water. "Life is shorter than you think, my child, so don't squander your days. Make the most of them."

"I do."

"No, you don't. You went to the university to please your father, now what are you doing with your degree?" He didn't wait for an answer. "Nothing. You shop and come in at all hours of the morning. I see the schedule you keep. Not much of a life, if you ask me."

He maneuvered his chair to the picture window and glanced at the horizon. "You should aim higher. One morning you may wake up and find yourself without a purpose." He shook his head and lifted his arm to encourage Barbary to hug him. "Listen to me. I don't mean to nag."

Barbary went to her grandfather. Each time he spoke of her lack of a career drive, something pricked at her soul. Were opportunities passing by? "I love you, even when you lecture me."

"Your hair is like your mother's." His delicate touch moved a short ringlet. "Will you do me a favor?"

"If I can."

"Think about what I said. Look deep in your heart." He wheeled over to his audio player. "Why don't you go visit my favorite place in Asheville? Take your camera and snap some of those self-photo things you young people do. I can put them in the album with my older pictures from the region."

Without answering, Barbary closed his door and ambled past a life-sized statue of a man in armor.

~ * ~

The next morning Barbary stood in the dining room, sipped coffee and stared out the patio doors at the white prairie clover. Footsteps made her turn from the scenery. Her father rushed into the room. She glanced his way while he buttoned the jacket of his navy-blue suit.

"Morning, Father."

"You were deep in thought." He poured a cup of coffee, took a drink and made a face. "Contemplating your latest fashion dilemma, I suppose?"

"Not hardly. I'm reflecting on the rest of my life."

"There is a place for you at the lab. We can always use someone with your degree in our biochemical department to design print and digital platforms."

"We've gone over this too many times. I don't want to work there."

"I can't understand why not. Nukerson happens to be the reason you have a country club membership and a limitless credit card. Perhaps you should think before you badmouth our existence. Your grandfather would say, 'don't bite the hand, which feeds you.'"

Barbary pursed her lips together to stop words of rebuttal, which would only prolong the discussion about her shortcomings. "Speaking of Grandfather, he asked me to take a trip to North Carolina and take some pictures for him."

"Really? He talks about North Carolina often. A dream of his youth, if you ask me..." He stopped short when the cook entered. "Mia. This coffee is foul tasting. What's wrong?"

"Sorry sir, they were out of your usual brand." The cook lowered her head.

"Nonsense!" Toss these distasteful coffee beans out. Get the proper kind." He slammed his cup down. "Now."

"Yes sir." She glimpsed at Barbary and left.

"Barbary. If you must, go visit the desolate land your grandfather speaks about. Perhaps, you'll realize where your career should be."

Barbary ran her hands over her arms, shook to break free from his words and hurried upstairs.

"Grandfather?" Barbary knocked on his door.

"What's wrong?" He sounded worried when he opened the door.

"Nothing." She looked at him in his wheel-chair noting an afghan over his legs. "Are you feeling well today?"

"I woke with a bit of a chill in these old bones. In a few hours I'll be fine. I'm waiting on Mia to bring me a bowl of cinnamon oatmeal."

"Father sent her to the store. I'll get you it. Remember, Mia taught me to cook."

"I do recall I like a little cream added."

"Not a problem. I'll be right back with breakfast." She turned to leave and looked over her
shoulder. "I almost forgot. I'm planning to go to
Asheville. I'll leave tomorrow if I can get a flight."

"Wonderful." His crow's feet deepened.
"Take plenty of pictures."

~ * ~

Barbary yawned. Surprised the short time difference from New Mexico to Asheville, North Carolina slowed her system down. She secured the key
card from her suite at Bellmore Gardens and walked
into the sitting lounge.

The long hallway supplied elevators to the
four stories of luxury suites. Twenty-foot ceilings
with chandeliers and hand carved columns accented
the lavish furnishings.

Barbary glanced at the detailed crown mold-
ing. Her father may not approve of the mountains
tucked back in Asheville. He would appreciate the
accommodations. She ambled toward the double
glass doors.

"Ma'am, would you like a brochure with a
map to help navigate the gardens." A hostess offered her a pamphlet.

"Thanks. I'm going to take a path down to one
of the flower gardens."

"Wonderful, follow the brick path. The trail
takes you directly to our most popular display, a
large bed of tulips."

"I'll be sure to find them."

An enormous acreage of red, yellow and pink
tulips surrounded the area. Remembering how much
her grandfather enjoyed flowers, she reached for her
phone to capture the vibrant shades.

Barbary turned to get a different angle of the multi-colored tapestry and took a few steps sideways to focus. Her foot landed on a hard object. The mass moved and caused her balance to falter, and she began to fall.

Her body came within inches of tumbling atop a man working the sod. "Oh my!" She moved quickly as a pair of rough hands caught her.

Barbary scrambled from the stranger's grip, turned and came chest level to a blue sport shirt with a Bellmore logo. She followed the insignia to large tanned biceps the color of burnt sienna. Her gaze moved upward to see coal black hair tied back at the nape of his neck and hung slightly below his shirt collar.

"You are in my way." Her eyes slanted. "I almost stepped on you."

"Or I stopped you from falling." He pointed toward the dirt. "I'm transplanting *Tulipa Gesneriana.*"

"What?"

"Tulips." He grinned. "*Tulipa Gesneriana* is the scientific name."

"I see." She tried to look away from his hypnotic but playful cocoa eyes. "Digging holes tourists may fall into isn't safe."

He raised a brow. "Applying plant fertilizer. And you stepped on me." The corners of his mouth twitched.

"I beg your pardon." Barbary moved back. "I didn't step on you. You tripped me." She turned and hurried to put distance between them.

"Name's Trace," he called. "In case you want to stumble over me again."

She picked up her pace and trotted toward the rose garden. Huge bright red blooms greeted

14

her, and she took a deep breath. The image of her encounter with the dark-haired man overshadowed the surrounding beauty. "Trace," she repeated his name. *He may be nice looking, but I won't speak to him again.*

Two

*T*race leaned back in his Adirondack chair, inhaled the mountain air and raised his glass of tea as if cheering the clouds. Hills and a small lake peacefully rested before him. Overhead, a white cloud leisurely hovered and brought memories of his father. Dad always believed the Upper World lived beyond the sky, in a place where the guiding spirits dwelled. He took a breath. "Dad's misguided beliefs." He cleared his throat. *Memories are all I can cling to.*

He took a drink of tea and dwelled on the years since his dad passed, and his mother relocated them off the reservation to Asheville. He could have never imagined a simple move would challenge his attitude. Sometimes, people could be worlds apart.

His focus shifted to the woman he met earlier. Trace ran his hand over his face attempting to wipe away the picture of her dimpled chin and electric-blue eyes, which seemed to zap him with a lightning bolt when she looked his way. *If looks could kill.* He chuckled, picked up his cell phone and tapped the screen, determined to forget the encounter with the pretty woman.

"Mom, how did your appointment go?"

"Trace," she stretched out his name. "The doctor gave me a good bill of health. I only have a cold. You'll have me around a bit longer."

"I'm glad. Are we on for our weekly dinner and Bible study?"

"Sure. I'm enjoying our study in the book of John."

"Me too. I was enjoying the nice day and Dad crossed my mind."

"I remember him often, too. I can't believe he's been gone so long."

"A month before my twelfth birthday. Dad used to tell me about the guiding spirits in the Upper World."

"He also believed in the Under World, where evil lives. You father related the similarity between his religion to Heaven and Hell. When he and I got married I tried to sway him toward Jesus.

I never gave up and never stopped praying."

Trace picked up a leaf. "Somehow, you two made things work."

"Yes, still, my parents gave me a hard time because I married an Indian. Your father's mother acted the same toward me. After he died, I thought you and I needed a fresh start."

"You did what you could." He tossed the foliage over the railing.

"I dislike the way some folks act toward a person who isn't like them. I wish more people would heed the teachings of Jesus Christ and be kind to each other."

"This would be a nicer world." The timer went off, signaling dinner. "I'll pick you up tomorrow evening at five."

"Wonderful, son." He slipped his cell into his pocket.

~ * ~

Two days later, Trace gathered his tools, pulled the blueprint from his clipboard and smiled at the finished construction of the newest pergola at Bellmore Estate. Now he could create an array of Dahlias to entice visitors to relax under the shade. He finished loading his cart.

When lunch arrived, Trace checked the progress made on the Dahlia Garden and smiled at a few guests who greeted him. He couldn't stop himself from searching for a certain blonde visitor. The memory of preventing her fall still vivid. Surely, the woman had left by now to go back to wherever she belonged.

I'll never know her name.

Three

Barbary walked slowly through the acreage of Bellmore. After a couple days of relaxing in the spa, she planned to tackle more sightseeing. She tapped her phone and took a snapshot of the French-style mansion, which served for the main attraction. Even with several postcards to take back to her grandfather, she figured he would want some real scenes.

She glanced at the time on her phone and noted he would be awake, most likely listening to an audio novel. Barbary tapped the phone to call New Mexico.

"Mia, please ring Grandfather."

"Yes, Ma'am. I hope you're enjoying the trip."

"I am. Thank you."

"Barbary," he sounded pleased. "How wonderful you called."

"I'm taking plenty of pictures. You were correct, this is a beautiful area."

"I told you."

"How's Dad? I'm afraid I left him on a sour note."

"He hurried off early for a meeting. He paused momentarily. Don't worry about your dad, he may be opinionated but he's a survivor. He's stubborn and likes things one way."

"Yes, his way. I get tired of our quarrels, and this place has offered a peaceful escape." She eyed the paths and bright plant life before her. "I may stay here a few more weeks. Maybe being away will soften Father. Tell him I called."

"Will do my child, and you don't need to hurry home. Have a good time at my favorite spot."

"I plan to."

Barbary eyed her phone while she hurried down a designated walkway and collided into a parked golf cart. "Ouch." She rubbed her head.

"You again?" Trace rounded the pergola and chuckled.

"I fail to see the humor in my bumping into this buggy you dangerously parked in the way. I should report you."

"Me?" Trace shook his head. "Lady, you're clumsy. This is the second time you've crashed into something, it's a wonder you haven't gotten yourself killed before now."

Barbary's huffed and planted her fists on her hips.

Trace pressed his lips together and paused. "I have no right to call you clumsy, I'm sorry. Name's Trace Youngbird, managing horticulturist." He held out his hand and smiled.

She hesitated and then grinned. "Pleased, I'm sure."

Barbary eyed the way his shirtsleeves dug into his biceps when his arm moved. His touch rugged and strong, not like the hands of the usual pencil pushers she dated. "Isn't Youngbird an Indian name?"

"Eastern Cherokee,"

"Barbary Willis. From New Mexico." She glanced at the way the sun shone on his hair. Intriguing and attractive, he made her stomach lurch like she was on a tall Ferris wheel.

"Barbary, I'm delighted to make your acquaintance. Would you like a guided tour later this evening?"

"I can get one of those anytime Mister Youngbird."

"Yes, but I promise to show you some attractions only the locals get to see. And please, call me Trace."

"Trace." She glanced away in indecision. Her grandfather would love behind-the scene photos. "What time is your tour?"

"Meet me in front of the inn in three hours."

"Okay." She turned and hurried in the direction of the tulip garden.

~ * ~

The sun moved nearer the mountains and the rays softened. Barbary took in the view from the bench in front of the inn. She glanced to her left and saw Trace coming.

He hopped off the golf cart. "Are you ready for a treat?" He held out his hand to help her to her seat.

"I hope you don't mind but I promised my grandfather I'd take pictures." She held up her phone. "He's no longer able to travel."

"Of course." He hurried to his side of the cart and steered behind the building. "I'm going to show you a few of the inner workings at Bellmore." He went over a hill and parked in front of a domed building. "This is the greenhouse."

Barbary took off her sunglasses and examined the huge circular building. "Is this where all the flowers come from?" She aimed her phone and took a shot.

"Producing them on the grounds is easier than ordering new plants every spring." We also grow veggies served in the dining room."

"You mean those sweet carrots I enjoyed at dinner came from here?"

"Sure did." He gently placed his hand on her arm and led her to the hothouse.

"This is huge."

"The area expanded over the years, used to be a ten by twelve structure."

Barbary walked beside Trace while he pointed out various plants, explaining each one. She fanned her face with her hand to displace the heat while they toured the facility.

They stepped back outside. Barbary matched Trace's steps down a path to a wooden building resembling a barn. A plank door led to dozens of wine kegs.

Trace motioned to the left. "Our winery. Bellmore uses a house specialty made here." He nodded to an older man. "Jimmy, this is Barbary. I'm giving her a special tour."

"Wonderful." The man patted his protruding stomach and smiled. "I'll let you sample our newest stock." After a moment, Jimmy returned with two glasses. "Try this."

Barbary touched the goblet to her lips. "Very good." She took another sip. "Doesn't taste like any wine I've had before."

"What we hope for." Jimmy twirled the corner of his long mustache. "Our specialty is only for the inn. We do sell a limited supply in the gift shop."

"Thanks, Jimmy." Trace gently took Barbary's arm and led her outside.

"Do you like?" He motioned to her glass.

"Yes. I'd love to take some back to New Mexico."

"I'll make sure the gift shop holds a bottle."

They strolled back to the cart. Barbary took her seat and placed her empty wine glass beside her. She touched Trace's arm. "I want to take a selfie." She held her phone up in front of her face. Trace moved sideways to get out of the frame. "No, let's do this together." She leaned close and adjusted her phone for a wide angle. "Thanks. Grandfather would like you."

"Really?" Trace rubbed his chin. "Why?"

"Grandfather is down to earth. He likes mountains and the simple things in life." She noticed Trace lifted a brow. "No disrespect intended. My grandfather values honesty and hard work. You seem to represent those ideas."

"I'm sure I'd like your grandfather, too." Trace grinned and headed the cart back to the inn.

When they reached the front door, Barbery scooted out of the golf cart. "Thanks for showing me an insider's view of the grounds."

"My pleasure." Trace ran his hand through his hair. "Would you join me in the dining room? I'm not dressed in fine attire, but their accommodations suit anyone's needs."

"I am hungry after our walk."

"Great." He got out of the cart and held out his arm. "Prepare your taste buds for a delight."

Barbary laughed. "I know. The meals are delicious."

They strolled to the restaurant on the east side of the inn. A sunburst with white clouds was etched on the stain glass window.

Once inside the hostess grinned. "Trace, good to see you."

"Ginger." Trace looked ahead at the tables. "Could we have a table for two, preferably in the corner?"

Barbary eyed the woman and wondered why her attitude toward Trace rubbed her the wrong way. For some reason, she wanted to slap the smile off the perky, bleached blonde's face.

"Certainly, follow me."

They made their way past a few tables to one against a floor to ceiling window. The hostess handed them menus. "Someone will take your order shortly." She tossed her hair over her shoulder and hurried away.

"This is a pretty view." Barbary looked out at a hillside displaying daisies made into a happy face.

"I thought you'd enjoy the flowers. Each dining area in the corners of the rooms," he nodded to the other side, "have a unique flower garden feature."

"Very nice." Barbary met Trace's eyes. For a few seconds she was mesmerized by the pools of rich, warm chocolate. She picked up her menu to break the spell but glanced over the top at a few wayward strands of his hair lying over his collar.

"What looks good to you?" Trace placed his menu aside.

You do. She grinned and said, "I'll have the Parmesan Gnocchi."

"I like the Blue crab they serve, too. Would you like a glass of wine?"

"No, thanks. Too much wine and I'll get a headache. I'll take some of your southern tea."

"I like wine but only on occasion." He nodded.

"You drank a glass of wine earlier."

"I know, for a special occasion."

24

"Why?" Barbary entwined her fingers on the table.

"You were by my side."

The waiter took their order and left. Barbary leaned back. Soft earth tones made the dining area relaxing, if only the butterflies in her stomach would leave by the time the meal arrived.

"I don't often visit such an interesting place."

"Asheville. A mountain town?" He reached for his glass. "I figured you for a world traveler."

"I've never visited such a quaint, laid-back area." She took a sip of her tea.

"You mentioned your grandfather. Did he live here?"

"For six months. He is fond of this part of North Carolina."

"I can see why. The place gets in your blood." The waitress set their plates on the table and Trace picked up his fork. "I hope you won't mind me saying a blessing?"

"I don't suppose." Barbary looked at Trace bow his head. She closed her eyes and listened.

"Heavenly Father, bless our meal and open Barbary's eyes to all Your beauty. Amen. Mom raised me to give thanks."

"She sounds like a wonderful lady."

"I think so."

After finishing her meal, Barbary pushed her empty plate to the side. "Thanks for dinner."

"I enjoyed the company." The corners of his eyes twitched. "Would you like to try some dessert?"

"No, thank you. I'm full."

"Do you feel like taking a walk? There's an area with some nice night-bloomers below the gazebo." Trace stood and scooted his chair back under the table.

"Night-bloomers?"

"Yes, Ipomoea alba, Brugmansia and Gardenia Augusta, to name a few."

"What?" Barbary stood and hung her purse over her shoulder. "Will you speak English?" She laughed.

"Sorry, when I discuss vegetation my horticulture nature comes out." He opened the exit door for her. "Moonflower, Angel's Trumpet, and Gardenias."

"Oh, here did you get your degree?"

"I went to college near Asheville, and during my last two years I interned here. After I graduated, they offered me a position I couldn't turn down. What about you?"

"I went to the University of New Mexico and studied Graphic Design."

"Interesting field, I'm sure." They companionably beside one another.

"Might be. I haven't started my career yet."

"Why not? I'm sorry. I don't mean to pry."

"No problem." Barbary shrugged. "I'm a little restless, I guess."

"One day you'll decide to try a new path in life."

"You think so?" Barbary slowed her pace to match his.

"We all reach a time in our lives when we want a change." He gestured to a well-lit area outlined in multi-colored lights. "Over there."

They walked under a long arbor adorned with foliage.

"Look at those heart shaped leaves on the big white flowers. They're beautiful."

"Moonflowers," he said and touched her hand. "This way. Smell the fragrance coming from the other white flowers? They're Gardenias."

"Sweet smelling." Barbary grasped his hand and admired the flowerbeds. "Reminds me of lemon."

"Let's sit." He led her to a bench.

"Those yellow and peach colored flowers are lovely."

"Angel's Trumpet. They take a lot of care," he explained and glanced at Barbary.

"Thank you for bringing me here." She turned and their noses almost touched.

Barbary gasped and suddenly rose from her seat. "I should get back to my room. I'm, um, I'm tired."

"Let me escort you."

They walked in silence. Barbary touched her mouth at the memory of his lips only inches from hers. *How would his kiss feel?*

Four

*B*arbary walked through the front entrance. "I learned a few things this evening."

"I didn't mean to bore you." He touched her arm. "I forget not everyone likes plants."

She smiled. "You didn't bore me."

"Maybe, I'll see you again." His eyes locked with hers. "When are you going back to New Mexico?"

"I don't have a schedule. Before I left, Father and I exchanged some words. I'm in no hurry to pick up where we left off. I may stay a few weeks."

"Will you do me the honor of going out again?"

"I might." She smiled and walked away.

Barbary stepped into the elevator, trying to recall the last time she'd enjoyed such an unpretentious few hours with a man.

~ * ~

Trace made his way home, visions of the blonde-haired woman whipped in and out of his imagination like a fast car changing lanes. He parked and relived the moment their faces were close. *Her lips looked soft.*

When he ambled into his living room, the answering machine blinked. Trace listened to Mom's stressed voice and dialed her number.

"Are you okay? Your message sounded odd."

"I'm fine, worried about you. I've been trying to reach you for hours."

"I'm sorry." Trace pulled his cell from the holder. "I turned my phone off."

"You hardly ever."

"I know. I escorted a guest around Bellmore, and we went to dinner."

"Are you responsible for the tourists now?"

"No." He rubbed his cheek. "Let's say we met under strange circumstances, and she's pretty and I... Never mind, long story."

"Hmm. I believe you like this lady."

"We were only enjoying one another's company. Besides, she's white and I'm an Indian."

"Trace Youngbird! You came from my womb, and I'm a white woman."

He moved the phone from his ear to buffer her tone. "I've been there too many times. Either the woman, or her parents, dislike my heritage."

"I'm sure this lady didn't have to go to dinner with you. It doesn't sound like your heritage is a problem."

"Anyway, she's from New Mexico, which adds new meaning to a long-distance relationship." He attempted a chuckle.

"Son, don't get discouraged. God has a plan for you."

"I know He does. Sometimes, I get impatient." He took off his loafers. "I should go. I have an appointment with a landscaper early in the morning."

"I love you."

"Love you too, Mom." He ended the call and headed to his bedroom.

~ * ~

The morning sun peaked over the mountains. Trace nodded to the contractor, proud of the newest addition to the gardens. A pond surrounded by cattails and lotus would be pleasing to the visiting tourists. He closed his office door, loaded tools onto his

golf cart, and grabbed the plans for the new fish enclosure.

The morning seemed to fly by, and when
lunchtime approached, Trace steered the cart toward his office, passing a blonde-haired woman sitting under a trellis reading. He took a second look
and turned the cart around.

"Hi, Barbary." He spoke over the engine clat-
ter and turned off the ignition.

"Hello." She eyed the cart. "I see you're busy
today."

"I finished marking a spot for a new attraction, a pond with a few Koi."

"I remember Mom's aquarium. I enjoyed
watching the fish swim."

"They say fish calm the nerves." He scooted
from his seat. "Always makes me relax when I see
them. I also like to catch trout for dinner." He
laughed and took a seat beside her.

"You fish?" She closed her book.

"Doesn't everyone?"

"Not me. And I've never been around anyone
who does."

"I see. I'll bet I'm different from anyone
you've met before."

"You seem like a nice man, since I've come to
know you a little better." Barbary laid her hand between them.

"Thanks." His dark hand touched hers. "You
have beautiful skin, the color of a lily."

"I don't tan. Even when I try, the color fades
too quickly." Barbary looked down at his long fingers. "You have a wonderful caramel tan." She laid
her other hand over his.

His eyes crinkled with happiness. "Do you have dinner plans? I have trout from my pond in the freezer. The cook at the inn will prepare us a meal."

"You have a pond?"

"Yes, and several acres not too far from here, pales in comparison to all this though." He nodded toward the grounds. "Still, I like the place. What about dinner?"

"I'd like to sample your trout." She pushed a strand of hair behind her ear and grinned.

"Good." He looked at his watch. "I have things to attend. I'll meet you in front of the inn at six."

"I'll be there."

He got back on his cart, headed in the other direction and waved.

~ * ~

Trace stood in front of Bellmore Gardens and watched the visitors come and go. He felt a soft hand touch his arm.

"Hi"

He smiled when he saw the sparkle in Barbary's eyes "You're lovely."

"Thank you. You look different tonight." She stepped closer and lightly touched a button on his shirt.

"I hope you approve." He glanced at her hand on his shirt.

"Definitely." She moved back, shocked at how comfortable she felt around him.

"Shall we go? I spoke with the cook earlier, and I'm sure our meal is almost ready." He held out his arm for her to take.

"We shall."

~ * ~

"We have a table waiting. Please, tell the cook the Youngbird party has arrived," Trace told the hostess and they went to their table.

When the meal was served, he placed his hand on the table, touched Barbary's fingers, and closed his eyes. "Lord, thanks for the fish you provided, and for the beautiful dinner companion. Amen." He opened his eyes and saw a rosy hue highlight Barbary's cheek.

"I like the company, too." She looked at her food and reached for a hushpuppy. "Mind if I ask you a question?"

"Go right ahead."

"I didn't realize Indians were religious, no disrespect intended. I'm only curious."

"I don't mind. My mother is white and my father was Eastern Cherokee. They each taught me their beliefs. Dad died many years ago, but he founded his assurances in the Upper World. I respect my heritage, but I grew up studying the Bible with Mom. Her Christian values stuck with me."

"What is the Upper World?"

"Many older Cherokees, and some younger ones, believe protective spirits live in the Upper World, and guide people in harmony. Like Christians, they have daily prayers and ceremonies. With the passing of time, I've witnessed many of my people turn to Jesus for salvation." He spooned tater sauce onto his plate. "God really leads our path, if we seek Him. Are you a believer?"

"I'm not sure." Barbary turned her glass around and wiped off the moisture. "Mom believed. I vaguely recall her taking me to Sunday school. She passed away when I was in grade school. Dad didn't have time to take me to church." She shrugged. "Life goes on."

"For me, a relationship with God helps smooth the edges of a trying situation. Like, when I have a bad day at work, I can't wait to get home and open my Bible. God's word gives me strength."

"You don't need bravery."

"I've overcame many things."

"I can't picture you in any position you can't handle."

"My heritage has caused friction. I've learned to accept some people's opinions of me when they see my dark skin. Sometimes, their ideas get mixed-up with common sense."

"I'm sorry." She lifted a brow. "Man, people."

"No fault of yours." Trace reached for her hand.

"I know. Still, I understand too well the kind of people you're talking about. Father is like many and can be a pompous butt sometimes." He belittles the cook because she's Spanish. I dislike narrow-mindedness." Barbary looked at their entwined fingers. "My grandfather is different. He likes people for who they are, and always speaks up for Mia."

"He sounds like a nice man."

"He is."

After the meal, they walked through the flower gardens. Trace held her hand while they strolled on a pebbled path toward a patch of day-lilies. He led her to a nearby bench. "Want to sit?"

"Yes." She took a seat and waited for him to join her. "This is nice."

"The plum colors are pretty." Trace looked around. "Smell that sugary fragrance? Night whispers are the common name for them."

"I didn't realize how much I enjoy the beauty around me until I came to Bellmore." She looked at the decorative foliage. "Also, sitting here with you is nice."

Trace slid closer to Barbary and put his arm over her shoulders. "I can't think of anyone I'd rather be sharing this view with." He lifted her chin with one finger. Lightly, his lips covered hers. "You're a special lady."

Trace rose from the seat and took her hand. "I should escort you back to the inn. I hope I wasn't too forward. I'm not the kind of man who romances just for the chase. But you're the first woman in a while to take the time to get to know me without judging."

They walked back to Bellmore and Barbary took his arm. "You weren't forward. I'm also used to being treated in a certain way. My family is prominent. Men tend to believe I'm only a shallow party girl."

"I would never think you were a superficial woman. I can see you're *a-ga-ta-hna-i*."

"A what?"

Trace laughed at her reaction. "It's a Cherokee phrase for wise."

She stood on her toes and kissed his cheek. "Goodnight."

~ * ~

The next morning, Barbary went the bathroom to wash her face, but her mind kept drifting to Trace. His dark hair reminded her of black silk as she recalled her lips on his warm cheek. She'd never lost herself in a man's caress before.

Shaking her head at such nonsense, she walked out to the grounds. Pretending to seek the biggest blooms on the rose bushes, as she glanced around searching for a handsome dark-haired man.

She watched several workers on the grounds, but none were the one she sought.

Barbary fingered a bloom, her mind traveled the miles to New Mexico, to her father and grandfather. "I'll be leaving shortly, anyway." She exhaled and reached for her phone.

"Mia, good afternoon,"

"Hello. Are you still having a good time?"

"Indeed. Is Father there?"

"Yes. I'll get him."

"Thanks."

Seconds later, a brass voice filled the silence. "Barbary, what are you up to?" His superior tone stung her ears.

"I'm enjoying my vacation," she said through clinched teeth."

"Yes, well, I imagine you're bored from the rural terrain by now. I've arranged an interview for you at the laboratory next week. An opportunity is opening up. You can't dismiss this chance to secure your place in society and continue the important work your mother and I began."

His idea of a future. She rubbed her temple. "Cancel the appointment. I won't be home next week. You're right about one thing, I do need to expand my world. When I return, I'm going to make plans to use my graphic design degree in Santa Fe."

"What? Your education will be better utilized at Nuckerson."

"I want to enjoy my work and create Internet advertising or paper ads."

"Humph. Sounds like a frivolous endeavor."

She frowned and tapped her toe on a knot of grass. "Being here and seeing all the beauty around me inspires me to design eye pleasing content. Not make charts about molecules, particles, or tragic life altering events."

A loud breath mimicking an approaching storm met her ear. She stood straight, prepared for the same wrath he often showed the cook when he was displeased.

"Young lady, you'd better be glad you have our privileges, otherwise you'd be living somewhere in squalor. How do you expect to survive in the fashion you're accustomed to on an advertising geek's salary?"

"Father, look around you. There are many people who are happy with less than we have."

"In your dreams!"

"I'm not going to quarrel. I have my mind made up. I'll make my own decisions."

"Perhaps, but don't come crawling to me when you can't afford to indulge your every whim. This may very well be an adventure and a mistake."

Barbary swallowed hard when he hung up on her. Determined not to let her Father's attitude dampen her spirits, she concentrated on the grass. *I'll stay a while longer. Hopefully, they'll hire someone quickly.*

A hand touched her arm. She jumped and turned to see Trace.

"Are you okay?"

"I will be." She wiped a tear from her cheek.

"Come here." He gently pulled her to him and closed his arms around her.

She leaned into him and let out a shaky breath, relaxing in his comforting embrace. After a few minutes, she put space between them. "I'm sorry."

"For what? You're obviously upset." He lifted her face to him. "Care to share? I'm a good listener."

She bit her lip with indecision. "Family concerns."

"Is your grandfather all right?" He led her to a bench and took a seat next to her.

"He's fine. Father is insistent about me working at Nuckerson Laboratories."

"I've heard about that facility. Isn't it a security research center?" Trace took her hand in his.

"Yes, and a major employer in the Los Alamos area. They design weapons to keep our country's security strong. The whole town thrives because of the scientific studies they do."

"I've read a few articles." He nodded. "I take it you can't see yourself being part of the company."

"No." Barbary shook her head and turned to face him. "Since I've been here and toured the grounds, I've realized I want to use my degree to create beautiful things. Not sit in a lab making charts."

"Your father should be happy with your decision."

"Father thinks any career not following in his footsteps is beneath me. He's set in his ways and says if I choose such an inconsequential job I'll be sorry." She glanced at some yellow roses and then back at Trace. "I'm a grown woman. I can make my own decisions."

"Barbary, do you mind if I do something for you?"

"What?"

"I want to pray for you concerning this situation."

"Really, you think prayer makes a difference?"

"Always helps when you get the Lord involved." He bowed his head. "Holy Father, we humbly seek Your guidance to tender the heart of Barbary's father. Give him understanding to respect other people's choices. Pave a way for Your grace in all that Barbary attempts. Amen."

She brought her head up. "I can't imagine Father being kindhearted about this."

"God can direct so things work out." He kissed her hand. "You need to believe. Can you?"

"I don't know. Father's stubbornness is a tough situation to deal with."

"One thing the Lord does in His time is to pave a way for the impossible to be possible." He touched her hair. "Stay strong and be open to what God can do."

"I'll try." She grinned half-heartedly.

"Good." Trace stood. "Can we have dinner tonight?"

"No." She caught a look of sadness cross his face. "I have a spa appointment and promised to return a few phone calls. I won't turn down a nice walk afterwards."

"Great. I'll meet you in the lobby about eight." He held out his phone. "May I have your number in case I'm running late? I never know when things will take longer than expected."

She took his phone and tapped the keypad, handed it back to him and smiled. Trace grinned, jumped into the cart, and waved.

~ * ~

Barbary pulled the spaghetti straps of her top in place, grabbed a brush and her cell, then pressed her home number. Three rings later, Mia's voice answered.

"Hello?"

"Mia, are you all right?"

"Yes, only putting a roast in the oven. Your father shut his office door with instructions not to bother him for anything until dinner. I don't mind saying, he's being a bear this evening."

"My fault, I'm afraid. Father and I didn't have a pleasant chat earlier."

"No worries. I'm used to his moody ways." The cook lowered her voice. "Is everything okay?"

"Wonderful. I think I've found determination to do something other than spend my days shopping."

"This is good," Mia said. "I must see to dinner."

"Of course. Please, get Grandfather for me." She brushed her hair and counted two rings.

"Are you still enjoying the mountains?"

"They're very nice." Barbary laid the brush on the counter. "I'm happy I came. The beauty of this place motivates me."

"Asheville is beautiful. I hope you have pictures."

"I've taken a lot of snapshots." She recalled the selfie with Trace. "I met someone who makes touring the grounds fun, too. He showed me the inner workings of the greenhouse and winery. Everything's nice." She sighed.

"Seems to be." He laughed, then loudly cleared his throat.

"Grandfather, what do you mean?"

"I detect more than a fondness for your sightseeing partner. You enjoy this tour guide's company?"

"Sometimes, I think you understand me better than I do myself." She walked onto the balcony. "His name is Trace. He's half Cherokee Indian." Barbary scanned the gray horizon and spoke about Trace Youngbird.

Thirty minutes later, she added, "Fantasizing about what might be, is fun, but I'll be home in New Mexico and he'll be here."

Grandfather's tone softened.
"Anything is possible. If you want to, you can make a way."

"Another daydream." She went back inside. "Father would have a royal fit if he knew I kept company with Trace."

"You mean someone who may have a different background? He would." Still, time comes when we must spread our wings. You can't please everyone. You need to make yourself happy."

"You're right." She slipped on her flats. "I've finally realized what direction I want my career to take."

"Do tell."

"One of the options graphic designers have is to combine art and technology to build websites, logos, and product illustrations." She highlighted a few ideas about utilizing her degree within the artistic pursuits.

"I'm intrigued. Tell me more."

"I will later. I should go now. Trace and I are touring more of the area."

"Very well." His pleasant, broken chuckle met her ears. "Be happy. However, I hope to see you back here for my birthday in a few weeks. This one is a milestone. Makes me look back and ponder my eighty years. Don't waste life. Move some mountains. Good bye, dear."

"We'll talk later, Grandfather."

Barbary slipped her key card in the pocket of her walking shorts and strolled to the lobby. She ambled over to the floor to ceiling windows and glanced at the overcast sky. The prayer Trace lifted to the Lord came to mind.

She gazed at the clouds and whispered, "God, do you remember me? I used to go to Living Life Worship, with Mother. Will you hear Trace's prayer? Grant me the ability to follow my heart." She looked down at the bow on her shoe. Questions sprang into her mind. *Why would the Lord give me favor? I'm not following His ways.*

Barbary looked up and spied a rack toward the end of the lobby. She started toward the display to find the perfect birthday card to celebrate her grandfather's milestone.

Six

Barbary paid for the card, tucked it into her purse and turned. From across the room Trace nodded in greeting and walked toward her.

"Hi. You're lovely."

"Thanks." She felt her checks grow warm.

"Are you ready for a walk, my lady?" He held out his arm in a courteous fashion

"Yes." Barbary laughed. They matched each other's steps toward the door and went outside. Barbary peeked at the sky. "The clouds look dark. Is rain coming?"

"I believe the weather channel called for a small chance, less than fifty percent." Trace pointed toward a mountain. "See the bare spot on the side of the mountain?"

"Halfway up the peak." She stretched her head and stared past the trees.

"Yep. My log home sits there."

"Not far." She continued to eye the countryside.

"Less than a mile. Do you want to take a short ride and check out my abode?"

She observed the rolling hills and debated. "I... guess."

"I want you to be comfortable. I understand if you don't feel at ease riding with me." He touched her shoulder.

Barbary pursed her lips from indecision. "I trust you." She smiled. "I'd like to see where you live."

She climbed into his truck and examined the inside of the vehicle. Another new adventure, riding in a pickup, the inside bounced more than her luxury car.

A house came into view. She eyed the A-frame roof and the long porch that circled the front. "This is your place?"

"Sure is. Wait." He got out of the truck, hurried to the passenger's side and opened her door. "I'll show you around."

They walked toward the house. A clap of thunder rolled, followed by a sudden downpour.

"Let's get inside." He shouted over the rain and put his hand on her back.

She ran toward the porch with Trace behind. Once inside, he hurried down the hall and came back with a towel. "You're wet."

"Thanks." She rubbed moisture from her hair and handed the towel back.

He tossed the terry cloth in the corner. "Come on. I'll give you the ten-cent tour."

Barbary eyed the far wall of windows, overlooking a pond. A stone fireplace dressed one side of the room. She examined the open-concept living space and ran her hand over the back of the leather couch. "You have a nice home."

"Suits me." He walked past the center island to the kitchen. "Please, have a seat." He motioned to the sofa. "Can I get you some tea?"

"Yes, thanks." She sat on the sofa. A sudden flash of lighting streaked through the window. She grabbed a decorative pillow and hugged it to her chest.

"This place is constructed to withstand storms." He motioned toward the windows. "Fair weather is what North Carolina is known for, here in the mountain region we often get snow, rain, and ice storms." Trace handed her a glass.

"Ice storms." Her eyes grew big. She looked away from the window, determined not to show any concern. Barbary slowly took a sip of her beverage. "This is good. You brew tea?"

"Most of the time, a bachelor needs to fend for himself." He laughed and held up his glass. "Mom likes to send me casseroles to hold me over, still, I do my fair share of cooking."

"I bake some. Mia taught me."

A faraway boom made her take a fast look at the door. Trace scooted close and put his arm around her. "Summer rains can be noisy. They'll be over shortly."

"I'll be glad." She laid her head on his shoulder.   For several minutes, she snuggled close, rain pelted down, and thunder reverberated through the mountains. Minutes late, the rain slowed. "I believe the worst is passed."

"Yes, the storm is gone." Trace hugged her and leaned down to capture her lips with his. Barbary ran her hand through his hair and welcomed his embrace.

He pulled back and smiled. "I'm glad you came to visit Asheville."

"Me too. You're not like anyone I've met before." She touched his cheek.

"I'm sure you don't meet many Cherokees within your circle of friends."

"I'm only saying you're a nice man." She pushed a wisp of hair from his brow. "And a good kisser."

"Really?" He lifted her chin. "Flattery will go a long way." He covered her mouth with his again.

Barbary never wanted this moment to end. She relished his touch.

Trace pulled back. "I think we should slow down." He reached for his beverage.

"Okay." She stared at him. "Trace, what happened?"

"What do you mean?" He looked at his glass.

Barbary leaned forward to gain his full attention. "We were enjoying each other's company and you stopped."

"You'll be leaving soon." He put his drink down.

"In a couple weeks. I'll need to be home for grandfather's birthday."

He leaned his head on her forehead and stared into her eyes. "Lovely lady, I wish you would never leave. If we could get to know each other better, I'm sure our relationship would grow into something beautiful."

"We can enjoy each other until I go." Barbary gazed into his dark eyes.

He stood, reached for her hand and gently pulled her to him. "I doubt we can have a long-distance relationship."

"I guess not. I'll never forget you, or the time we have together."

He hugged her. "I'll grieve for what might have been."

She touched his arm. "We still have two weeks."

"I'm a forever kind of guy. When I find a special someone, I want a committed relationship." He took her hand and walked with her to the door. "I'll enjoy our walks and dinners until you go. I honestly couldn't stay away from you unless you told me to. Now, I'd better get you back to the inn before the rain starts again."

Barbary mulled over Trace's words while he drove. His ideas certainly differed from any man she'd ever encountered. *Commitment, wow.*

She opened the truck door to get out. In a flash Trace stood by her side. "Thank you for a wonderful time." He hugged her.

"A rainy evening." She laughed.

"I can't think of anyone I'd rather be stranded with." Even though we won't have a chance for anything serious to happen between us, I would like to continue to get to know you while you're here. I have tomorrow off, how about a trip into Asheville? They have an art gallery I think you'd enjoy."

"Sounds nice." She stood on her tiptoes and kissed him before heading to her suite.

Seven

*T*race pulled down his driveway and hurried to the covered porch to flee from the heavy rain that began to fall again.

He pictured Barbary and eyed the sky. *Why Lord?* "Why do I still want to spend time with her when I know nothing can happen? I hardly know her, but I already care." He recalled his mom telling him God had a plan. "I wish you'd move a little faster." Trace shook his head. "I'm sounding ungrateful when I'm blessed in many ways." He sighed and went inside.

~ * ~

The next day Trace pressed Barbary's number. "Good morning." He looked at his wristwatch. "I hope I haven't called too early."

""No, I finished a nice breakfast delivered to me on the patio."

"Bellmore Garden will spoil you." He walked over to his window and gazed at the multicolored ring spread over the mountain. "The showers last night left a rainbow."

"I know. The pink colors seem so vivid."

"Do you know what the rainbow means?"

"Rainbows form because the sun shines onto droplets of moisture after a heavy rain."

Trace laughed. "You're right, at least scientifically. There's more though. Have you heard the story of Noah and the Ark?" After the great flood God made a covenant to never again destroy the earth with water. The rainbow is the promise of God's word. You'll find the story in the book of Genesis, chapter nine."

"I remember a little from Bible school. I recall God told Noah to build an ark, so his family and the animals would survive. When I see things from your perspective, they're much more gracious."

"What do you mean 'my perspective'?"

"A Christian."

"Oh. Sorry, sometimes I get a little paranoid because of my Indian heritage."

"I promise any snide comments I make will be because you're being pigheaded, not on account of your heritage." She laughed.

He chuckled. "Thanks for clearing things up."

"No problem. Now, when are we going to the gallery you mentioned?"

"How about I pick you up at eleven-thirty? We can have lunch at a nice bistro in town. I realize Bellmore's American bistro is good, but the one downtown serves French fare."

"Shall we meet in the lobby?"

"Yes, beautiful lady."

Trace ended the call and went back to his bedroom. He took a shirt from the hanger and eyed the button down, hoping to please the woman stealing his heart. *Lord, help me guard my feelings.*

~ * ~

Trace strolled through the lobby and found Barbary reading while sitting in front of the fireplace. She looked up and closed the book.

"You looked relaxed." He smiled and let his eyes roam from her gold ankle bracelet to her mint green, knee length dress.

"Very much." She glanced at the crackling fireplace. "There is something calming about a fireplace, even when you don't need the warmth."

"I agree." He took hold of her hand. "Still, they're better when there is a chill outside. I use mine a lot. Shall we go?"

Trace drove the few miles into the main section of Asheville. He glanced over at Barbary and silently reminded himself not to let her turn his emotions upside down. He parked in front of a small street side building. "This place might not be decorated fancy, but the food is a once in a lifetime experience."

Barbary looked from one end of the white cement building, to the other. She frowned at the stick drawings of cows and pigs. "I'll have to trust you."

"You can trust me in any situation." Trace wiggled his eyebrows.

"We'll see." A musical chuckle filled the truck.

"Wait. I'll help you." He hurried to her side, opened the door and took her hand to aid her to the pavement.

"Thanks. You truck is a bit much for my five foot-five inches." The corner of her mouth curved with happiness.

Trace put his arm out for Barbary, guided her into the bistro and secured a table.

The waiter placed menus in front of them. "May I get you some wine?"

Trace looked at Barbary. "Would you like a glass?"

She shrugged. "Only, if you're having some."

"I think tea will be fine." He watched the server leave and turned to Barbary. "We should enjoy some more of the estate's wine again."

"I agree."

The server returned with their drinks. "Sir, are you ready to order?"

Trace looked across the table at his dinner date. "Barbery, I'm thinking of having the Boeuf Bourguignon."

"The beef tips, mushrooms, and Cipollini onions do sound good."

"Great," Trace said. "Make it two." The waiter jotted down the orders, collected their menus and left.

Trace took a sip of his beverage. "I'm not a man who likes to play games, so I'm going to say what's on my mind."

"Okay." She laid her hand on her napkin and watched him.

"You don't need to give me the evil eye, I'm not going to be mean." He smiled. "I only wanted to tell you I really do care for you." He reached across the table and grasped her fingers. "You know I wish you didn't have to leave. If we spent more time together, I think we would discover we're meant to be."

"Wow." Barbary moved her hand. "I know you mentioned it, I still don't know how to comment."

"Do you like me?" He stopped talking when the server set plates before them.

Barbary waited until they were alone. "I do. You're a great guy."

"Thanks." He picked up his fork and grinned. "Mind if I ask a blessing?"

"Go ahead." She closed her eyes.

"Lord, bless our food and lead us to do Your will. Amen."

"What is," she picked up a roll, "God's will?"

"His desire is for us to glorify Him and be kindhearted toward one another. There is a verse in Matthew, chapter seven which says, 'So in every-thing, do to others what you would have them do to you, for this sums up the Law and the Prophets.'"

Barbary swallowed a bite and sat back in the chair. "Does the Bible instruct us in everything?"

"Yes, if we seek answers with an open heart." He secured a beef tip with his fork. "Sometimes, reading the Holy Word takes patience and prayer. His scriptures help us to live a better life." He smiled and chewed. A few seconds later Trace add-ed. "Are you enjoying the food?"

"Very much. I'm glad you invited me."

After their lunch, Trace escorted Barbary to his truck, and headed to a gallery in Asheville. Trace parked his vehicle "My lady, get prepared for some local culture." He got out of his truck and assisted her. "I know you've probably visited many galleries with exhibits from famous artists Hillside Made Gal-lery is known for local arts and crafts."

"All the displays are made here?"

"Sure are." He took her hand. "Let's go this way first. I'm saving the best for last."

Pottery of all sizes lined the glass shelves and counters. "This is beautiful. I like the blue and brown swirls." Barbary picked up the dish.

"A lot of work goes into hand crafting," Trace said, and ran his finger over the wavy pattern.

Trace marveled at the enjoyment Barbery got from learning about the local artists. He stopped be-side her and eyed a metal wall hanging of a twisted tree. "I feel like I grew up here. My mom brought me all the time. Seeing the crafts with you, gives me a new appreciation of what this place means to Asheville."

"Everything is beautiful." She paused at a basket and looked at maroon and green circles decorating the wicker. "The tag says, J. P. Bearpaw, is this name Cherokee?"

Trace nodded. "Many people from my Father's side have artistic talents."

"They certainly do." She strolled ahead and examined a wall tapestry.

"Let me show you what's in here." He nodded toward an area to his left.

Trace led her into a circular room. "The jewelry is from our locals in Asheville, and from the reservation." He watched Barbary move from one case to another and survey the necklaces, charms and earrings. After a few minutes, he joined her at a table.

"Trace, there is so much talent here. I've paid hundreds for necklaces not nearly this beautiful."

"Come with me." He gently took Barbary's hand and walked with her through a hall into a posh store. Barbary spied an owl necklace.

"This is very pretty." She touched the jewelry. "Look at the delicate wings and the feather details. I wonder how anyone can create such a lovely piece."

"Let me see." Trace picked up the jewelry. "I can tell you how this is made."

"Okay, do tell." She watched him.

"This owl," he held the figurine out, "is fashioned from a sheet of sterling silver, beat with a hammer many times, until smooth. The eyes are emeralds."

"Emeralds?" She took the jewelry and examined the green stones. "How do you know?"

"I have intimate knowledge." He took the necklace. "My mom makes these. Dad taught her years ago. The emerald is found here in Western North Carolina."

"It certainly is wonderful." She held onto the silver chain.

"Come on." Trace approached the service desk and slowly turned a small card rack around. "Perhaps, your grandfather would enjoy a few facts about our local pottery?"

"He would." Barbary picked out a card and scanned the information block describing a salad bowl.

"May I?" Trace laid the postcard down, added a couple more and grinned at the woman behind the counter. "We'll take these and the necklace."

"Wonderful choice." The cashier completed his transaction.

They strolled outside toward his truck. Trace took the gift box from the bag and removed the necklace. "Let me." He reached behind her and hooked the clasp.

"Beautiful, but you shouldn't have bought this for me."

He shook his head. "Please accept this. Let it represent a gift of appreciation for the times we've enjoyed." He lightly kissed her. "I also helped Mom. She gets a percentage from the sale."

He opened the truck door, waited until Barbary scooted inside, shut the door, then went to the driver's side. "Now my lady, may I educate you on the meaning of your necklace?"

"Sure. You're a wealth of knowledge." Barbary laughed.

Trace wrinkled his brow. "You're probably not interested."

"I am. I enjoy our conversations, they're interesting. Please tell me."

"Okay." He laid his arm over the seat. "I know you've heard the saying, 'the wise owl.' An owl is the symbol traditionally linked to knowledge. One night I while outside with my dad we saw an owl. He told me the bird is the link to wisdom and foresight. The charms are supposed to inspire someone to be more insightful

"Oh." Barbary laid her hand over the silver figure. "I suppose this gift is meant to be."

Trace leaned closer and feather kissed her on the cheek. "Why?"

"In the days to come, I'll need wisdom and confidence."

He quickly gave her a short kiss, and without a word, started his pickup and headed back to Bellmore Estates.

Trace walked Barbary to the front of the lobby. "Thank you for joining me."

"I enjoyed our time together. And Grandfather will be pleased to see these postcards from the gallery."

"From the few things you've told me about the man, he sounds like a good person." Trace put his arms around her. "May I ask you something?"

Eight

*B*arbary stared into his eyes. His breath graced her lips. The closeness hypnotized her. "Ask me anything."

"Will you consider coming back to Asheville after your grandfather's birthday?" He whispered in her ear.

"Trace, I'd be lying if I said I won't miss you too. If only things were different."

"I'm going to pray about us." He turned and walked away.

"Don't make this any harder," Barbary called. "Some things aren't meant to be."

~ * ~

Unbearable silence filled her ear. Barbary held the phone and squinted in the morning sun while she waited. Father would have Mia call and then make her remain on the line until he wanted to speak.

"Barbary?" His voice blared.

"I'm here." She sat on the patio chair and swung her foot.

"When will I expect you home? Your grandfather is having a birthday this weekend." His words sounded rushed. "Perhaps, you've joined yourself to Grandfather's mountain fantasy, and tossed us out of your life?"

"Father, you're being rude. I love Grandfather and will be home for his celebration." I know we have our differences, but I care for my family." She pinched the bridge of her nose. "And you're my father. I'll always love you."

"Hmm. Give some thought to your comment young lady. Maybe you'll realize since I am your father, I know best."

"What?" She shook her head. *I will not get into this with him today.* "I have to go. I have flight arrangements to make."

Barbary pressed end, narrowed her eyes at her phone, and dialed the number for the airport. Minutes later, she'd confirmed reservations for a return flight to New Mexico.

Still holding her cell, she replayed her days at Bellmore with Trace. She stepped inside her suite and searched out her flip-flops while her mind hung onto the image of Trace. Somehow he'd sneaked his way into her heart. Absent-mindedly, she pressed his number.

"Barbary, good morning." His jolly tone was welcoming.

"Hi." Is your day starting off on a good note?"

"So far. I arranged a schedule for the water trucks to fill up the pond. Hopefully, I can get the fish here before the summer season is over."

"The visitors will enjoy the scenery." She sat on the edge of the bed.

"I'm sure. Hey, I can tell you're bothered by something."

"How do you know?"

"Your voice doesn't have the positive tone I'm used to."

"I return to New Mexico on Friday."

"I see. I'm going to miss you something fierce."

"We have a couple of days." She shook her head. *Why did I say anything, things are hard enough?*

"My schedule is busy today. I would like to see you before you leave, how about tomorrow evening? Meet me around six, beside the tulips."

"Okay."

She tossed her phone on the bed and sighed at another one of her many bad decisions. Barbary took her suitcase from the closet and began to pack things she wouldn't need. She laid aside a comfortable traveling outfit for the flight home, wiped a tear and looked at her wet finger. *Crying.* She knew Trace less than a month. How could she care about him so much?

~ * ~

Barbary hurried to the flowerbed and sat down on the closest bench. She pulled her phone from her pocket and tapped the screen to capture a picture. She felt a hand on her shoulder and turned. "Trace." She jumped to her feet.

"Hi." He hugged her and gave her a heartfelt kiss. He pointed toward a bush. "See the new blooms."

"They're lovely." She stared into his eyes. "This is the place where we met. You tried to trip me." She laughed.

"Me?" He gently placed a strand of her hair behind her ear. "You fell for me, my beautiful lady."

She laughed. "You're right." Her smile faded. "I believe I have fallen for you. And we're so different."

"Not really, except for my heritage." He took her hand, and they sat on the bench together. "Even if you lived close by, your family would never give us their blessings."

"My Grandfather would." She laid her head on his shoulder. "You know what I've discovered since being in Asheville?"

"What?"

"My ideas of how I want to live are very different from Father's. No matter what I do, his opinions will create friction between us."

"Because your father wants you to follow in his footsteps." He kissed the top of her head.

"How do you break the mold?" Barbary looked at Trace.

"You find a way to be yourself, and still honor your family." He grasped her hand. "Mom says sometimes with misunderstandings all we can do is agree to disagree."

"She sounds like a smart lady." Barbary glanced at their entwined hands.

~ * ~

The dresser drawers were empty. Barbary checked the rest of the suite to make sure she packed all her belongings. A traveling outfit hung from the hook in the bathroom, her make-up laid on the counter. She placed her tote on the floor, ready to hold her cosmetics for the flight home. In eight hours, she would be on her way to New Mexico. Her cell phone buzzed, and she glanced at the contact.

"Hi, Trace."

"Hello, my beauty. Are you positive you want to spend your last day at my place fishing? We could go to a restaurant. I know a very nice place."

"I've never been fishing. Besides, you promised me a grilled steak."

"I went shopping yesterday and purchased the best ones in the store. I'll pick you up this afternoon."

"See you in the lobby later."

~ * ~

Barbary stood outside and snapped one last picture of Bellmore Estates. She looked up, focused on the patio, adjacent to her suite, and tapped her phone. A light touch made her turn around. "You're always sneaking up on me."

"Not intentionally, and only when you're busy taking pictures." Trace grasped her hand. "Are you ready to become an angler?"

"If angler means a person who can fish, I am." She followed him to his truck.

Sunlight skipped on top of the pond and the droplets of water twinkled like the stars in the night. Barbary stood at the edge of Trace's pond and studied the mountains. "You have a wonderful place. Do you mind?" She held up her phone.

"No, snap away. I have nothing to hide." He chuckled, picked up two fly rods and walked toward her.

"I'm ready." She put her phone down.

"I'll make this a fast lesson." He laid his lures on a rock. "I can't promise you'll catch a fish." He handed her a fly-rod and guided her hands. "Hold your fishing pole like this."

Barbary's stood stiff, determined to concentrate on the technique of fishing, and not the closeness they shared.

She let Trace placed his hands around her waist to show her the correct way to cast out the line. Barbary breathed in and paid attention to the lesson. "Are you sure this is how?"

"Of course," is cheek brushed against hers.

"Move like this and toss toward the deep part of the water." His body swayed while the line flowed across the pond.

"I did it." She laughed when the fishing line landed, turned and kissed him on the cheek. A tug on her pole made her jump. "I got one! What can I do?"

"Easy. Don't rush." Trace touched her wrist to help steer the line.

"I got this." She moved from his grasp, stepped sideways and stumbled. With another fast movement, she caught herself to keep from landing in the water. "Trace, the rod doesn't feel heavy like before."

"Let me see." He grabbed hold of the pole and shook his head. "Your catch got away."

"Dog-gone, I can't believe I lost my fish." She balled her hand into a fist.

"Don't be hard on yourself. Not many anglers get a fish on their first lesson." He picked up the bait. "Good job. You'll have to come back another day for lesson two." He draped his arm around her. "Come on. I have a steak to grill."

Barbary sat on the back deck, legs propped over the lowest banister rung. She sipped from a bottle of water while Trace grilled. "This is a serene place."

"Yeah." He turned over the T-Bone. "There's nothing like relaxing on the patio, looking out at the pond after a stressful day."

Minutes later, he placed the meal on their plates. "Anytime, you need to get away, you're welcome to sit on my back deck."

"I'm afraid I live a little too far away for an evening stroll."

She rose when she noticed him set the dishes on the patio table. When she approached her seat, he pulled out the chair. "Thanks."

"My pleasure." He seated himself, laid his hand on hers and bowed. "Heavenly Father, I ask You to bless this meal and to guide us. Thy will be done in our lives. Amen."

Barbary opened her eyes and grinned. "Do you really think the Lord guides us?"

"I do." Trace passed her the steak sauce. "The Lord knows what lays ahead, the good, and the bad. If we let Him be part of our life, He can lead us."

"God hasn't been part of my life," she said, cutting into a piece of meat.

"Everyone's been there, at one time or another. Jesus saves those with a sincere heart." Trace looked up from his plate, his face solemn. "When you're ready to learn more about Christ, read Romans, and remember I'm always here to talk."

"Okay." Barbary put a steak tip in her mouth.

When they finished the meal, Barbary helped Trace gather the condiments and leftovers and carried them inside. "I enjoyed the meal." She placed her glass in the dishwasher.

"I grilled and tossed a salad, nothing more." He took a bowl from her and circled her in his arms. "I'm fortunate God placed you in my life, even for a short time."

Barbary kissed him. The passion she experienced resembled a helium balloon lifting into the atmosphere.

"Trace, this isn't helping. I'm leaving for New Mexico in the morning."

His breath stroked her ear in a soft whispered. "Can we at least talk over the phone?"

"We can," she mumbled.

He exhaled. "Come on, I'll take you back to your room."

Barbary held the door handle when the truck came to a stop. Her stomach churned with the notion she'd never come back to North Carolina. She needed to make a clean break from Trace and end the relationship.

"Trace, I'll never forget these weeks we've spent together. Any woman would be fortunate to have you in her life." Quickly, she opened the truck door and eyed him. "Except, I'm not any woman. My life is in New Mexico. You belong in North Carolina."

He opened his mouth to speak, but Barbary didn't give him the chance. "No. There's nothing to say. Some things can't be changed and must be faced. This is my final goodbye." She slammed the truck door and rushed inside the inn.

Nine

*B*arbary left the baggage area of the airport and took slow steps to the curb. She cupped her hand over her eyes to block the sun, and gazed around, in search of the family driver. Her father's long, black town car pulled up. The chauffeur exited and hurried to load her suitcase.

"Thank you, Hector."

He opened her door and waited. "Very welcome, Miss Barbary." He hurried around the car and pulled into traffic to head home.

"I hope you enjoyed your vacation." Hector glanced in the rear-view mirror.

"I did. I guess," she mumbled.

The long driveway came into sight. Barbary took a quick look around the manicured lawn. A fountain flowing with water embellished the front yard. The rock formation stood stately positioned in the center. She had never before paid much attention to the four-thousand square foot home with extended terrace and adjoining gables.

Grandfather sat in his wheelchair on the balcony adjacent to his room. When the car stopped, he waved and wheeled inside.

The driver opened her door. "Would you like me to carry your bags upstairs?"

"Please, put them in front of my door." She walked towards the mahogany entryway and turned. "Thank you." She entered the house and jogged up the stairs to find her grandfather.

"Grandfather." Barbary hurried down the hallway.

"Did you have a good time?" He reached out and hugged her.

"I did. I'll come back in a little while and we'll chat. I have photos." She held up her phone. "I'm going to download them and print off a few."

"Wonderful." He straightened his lap blanket.

"Grandfather, is everything alright?"

"For now, we'll chat more this evening. I'm having dinner in my quarters. Come by later and bring a slice of Mia's Chocolate Lava cake with you. We can look at those pictures and enjoy dessert together."

"Okay. The time change tired me out. I'll see you after a while." She kissed his cheek.

Four hours later, Barbary sat on the edge of the bed and stretched after an invigorating nap. She pulled a blouse from the drawer, paired with linen slacks, placed them on the bed and headed to the shower.

The owl necklace gleamed in the mirror. She grasped the winged figure and closed her eyes. *Wisdom. I need to find my place in this world like grandfather said.* "God, I do need insight." Barbary opened her eyes wide. Surprised she addressed the Lord. She shook her head in wonder and stepped into the steaming shower.

Soon the copier hummed. Barbary duplicated snapshots from the file she'd downloaded from her phone. She picked up a photo, admired the rose garden at Bellmore Estates and several snapshots highlighting the mountains. She planned to place them on top of the stack. They would be her grandfather's favorite. The rest of the scenes from her travel landed in the printer tray while she typed the word, 'employment' into the search bar of her laptop.

Barbary logged into a well-known job-matching site. In no time, she loaded her profile and degree information, and checked a block to get employment alerts in email. She hit enter, ready to see what the world of graphic design offered.

Barbary stacked the postcards and pictures in a decorative box from the gift shop. A colorful scene of meadows and hills covered the lid. She placed everything next to her door to take to Grandfather's room later. A fast look at the time reminded her of dinner.

Barbary strolled into the kitchen. "Hi, Mia." She picked up a Mozzarella stick from the entrée platter.

"Miss Barbary. Now don't eat the appetizers." Mia shook her head and smiled. "Your father wants Italian."

"Sounds good." Barbary dusted crumbs from her hand.

"What did you do on your vacation?" The cook looked up from her duties.

"I took a lot of pictures for Grandfather and toured Asheville, North Carolina."

"And..." Mia washed her hands.

"And what?" Barbary looked at Mia.

"Ms. Barbary, you're very good with people. I can't believe you were gone for three weeks and didn't meet anyone."

"I did meet a nice man. He works there and gave me several tours." She stared at the stove. "He is very different from anyone I've been around."

"In a good way, I hope." The cook sliced the bread.

"Yes." Barbary nodded. "Is Father home?"

"Certainly, but he told me not to disturb him until dinner is ready." Mia shook her head. "His temper makes him act like a bear."

"I know." Barbary glanced toward the hallway. "Sometimes, I think Father doesn't know how to be any other way than moody."

"He wasn't always unbearable." The cook opened the refrigerator and took out the parmesan. "I think back to when you were young. Your father needs a companion."

"He often goes to the theater with Nadia Tisdale."

"She's too busy trying to please everyone and doesn't challenge your father. He needs a lady who will face his grumpiness." Mia nodded. "Your mother matched him perfectly. She used to tell me he needed his feathers bristled occasionally," she laughed, "I don't think he's ever gotten past her death."

Barbary glanced at the cook. Her mind raced back to her childhood. "Perhaps, you're right. Dad did seem easier to get along with in elementary school."

"Mark my word, child. If your father ever meets a woman who'll stand up to him, he'll be happier, even if he doesn't realize it. Now, go wash the cheese stick grease from your hands, so you can eat."

Minutes later, Barbary strolled into the dining room and gave Father a polite hug, before taking a seat. "I hope you enjoyed your day?"

"Outrageous." His boisterous tone rumbled across the table.

Barbary glanced at Mia, while she placed the meal on the table and left. "Why are you so annoyed?"

"The nerve of people never ceases to amaze me." He served himself a helping of baked Ziti. "The new communications facility coordinator had the audacity to correct me in front of a tester." He shoved pasta in his mouth and chewed vigorously. "She called my management skills prehistoric. The woman even used the term 'mulish'. I hope next time upper management hires a man." Give a woman a position of authority and they go wild. Women!"

Barbary stifled a grin. Her father's conversation made her remember Mia's comment about her mother. "What's her name?"

He put his fork down and eyed Barbary. "Regina. Does her name matter?"

"No. Only curious about the lady who fired you up."

"Fired me up? No longer than you were in North Carolina you've picked up their hillbilly lingo!"

Her voice rose, "Hillbilly... never mind." She took a breath. "I'll not speak with you about your misconceptions."

"My daughter," he pushed his plate back, "when you were in Asheville you told me you would seek employment beneath this family's station. I'm sure all this came about while sightseeing in those mountains."

Barbary wiped her mouth and tossed her napkin down. "For your information, being in Asheville only gave me clarity." She scooted her chair back. "I'm done. Maybe Regina is right about you." She couldn't get away fast enough.

~ * ~

Barbary gazed out of her window. The hue from the blue sky held a pinkish orange cast, as the day neared a close. *Did the horizon look the same in North Carolina? Wonder what Trace is doing?* She shook her head to displace any ideas of him, which begged for attention.

She moved from the window, grabbed the handle to the keepsake box she'd prepared earlier, and headed to the kitchen for the cake Grandfather mentioned.

Barbary entered the room. Mia placed two slices of cake onto saucers. "Is this for me?"

"Yes, your grandfather remarked you'd join him with dessert." The cook handed her the tray.

"Thanks. I'm sure we'll enjoy it." Do you believe people can rearrange their lives and be happier?"

"I do." The cook started the dishwasher. "A person's outlook makes the difference."

"What do you mean?" Barbary leaned against the cabinet.

"In my opinion, I believe someone can make things hard by not following God's light."

"I've never heard you speak about the Lord before."

"I know." Mia clicked her tongue and stared out of the window. "I guess I've let your father bully me for too many years. When your mom died, he instructed me not to talk of God around him." She walked closer to Barbary. "Thank goodness, your mom gave me her Bible for safe keeping. I can still recall the day the pastor stopped by after the funeral, and your father yelled and ran him off. I suppose he blamed the Lord."

Barbary gasped. "I wondered why the pastor never came to see us. Surely, Father doesn't think the Lord is responsible for Mom's Leukemia?"

"I believe he considers her faith in vain, since she wasn't healed." The cook wiped her hands on a paper towel.

"Mia, are Father's ideas right?"

"Absolutely not. We all need faith. To a certain extent everyone puts faith in things. Like when you're sitting in a chair." You have faith the seat will hold you. Only faith in God is more important than the worldly confidence people use. You mother's faith carried her through life and gave her the promise of security with our Lord. We all have a time to leave this world."

"Mia, may I see Mom's Bible sometime?"

"I've been waiting for you to ask." Mia grinned. "All these years, I've kept her Holy Book safe for you."

Barbary rearranged the tray and hung the keepsake box on her arm. "Thanks, I should take this to Grandfather."

She hurried up the stairs and approached her grandfather's half-open door. "Grandfather?"

He looked up from his writing. "Come in."

"I have our cake."

"Chocolate Lava, I hope." He wheeled to her.

"Yes." She set the dishes down

"Wonderful." Grandfather removed the napkin from around his fork. "I can't wait." He slid a bite into his mouth.

She took a bite and savored the rich chocolate. They ate in silence.

When Grandfather finished his dessert, he said, "Mia's cakes are always delicious." He leaned back in his wheelchair. "She's a wonderful chef. Your mother prepared a great meal, also."

"I remember her dinners." Barbary dwelled on his comment.

"Her passing caused a void in this family."

"Mia spoke earlier about how Father changed after Mother left us." Barbary opened the gift box she'd brought with her.

"Yes. For years, I tried to discuss things with him." Grandfather's wobbly hand moved a piece of hair from his face. "I'm afraid my meddling made him more belligerent. I gave up."

"Mia says he needs someone in his life." She took the photos from the keepsake box.

"Indeed." I believe your father deliberately keeps people at arm's length."

Barbary pondered her Grandfather's words and sighed. "I don't mean to change the subject, but I brought pictures.".

"Good, let's see." He leaned toward the table.

Barbary laid the stack of photos in front of him and began to explain their history. "Here's the view from the window of my suite at Bellmore Estates."

"I do remember how nice the sunsets were." He held the image and eyed the keepsake carton. "A box?"

She laughed. "I like the pretty, colorful scenery."

Grandfather grinned and studied the container. "Well made, for a cardboard box. I'll store these, and a few others pictures I have lying around."

"This is the winery at the estate." She pointed. "See those racks? They cover all four sides of the

room and are stacked to the ceiling with wine. I
sampled a glass It's very good."

He chuckled. "Did you by chance, bring one
back."

"I did." She leaned closer to Grandfather.
"Mia is chilling the bottle now. I told her to serve
you a glass before bedtime."

"Hot-dog." Grandfather slapped his knee.
"Thanks, Barbary."

She filled him in on her adventures while the
hour passed. Grandfather picked up a photo and
scrutinized the vacation memento. He eyed the man
beside Barbary. "Who's this nice-looking young man
sitting beside you?" He held the selfie out. "This
must be the man who gave you special tours."

"I meant to leave this one in my room." She
wiggled in her seat. The picture pulled at her heart.
"I mentioned Trace."

Grandfather slid the snapshot to Barbary.
"Yes, you said he was nice company."

"Did I?" She took the picture.

"Not in those words. I've known you long
enough to understand what you mean, and by your
reaction, I get a feeling this man left quite an im-
pression on you. Please, tell me about him."

She blinked several times with indecision. "He
is a wonderful man. Still, there are too many miles
between us for any kind of relationship. He told me
the day before I left, part of his heart would go with
me." She swallowed a lump. "Doesn't matter. I said
my final goodbye before my flight home."

"I see." Grandfather held the wheelchair arm
and exhaled. "Perhaps you need to open your eyes
to the possibilities life can hold."

"What do you mean?" She put the photo in
her pocket.

"If Trace says you have his heart, sounds serious to me." Grandfather eyed her. "How do you really feel about him?"

Ten

Barbary turned from her grandfather's gaze. "Trace is the first man I've enjoyed doing simple things with. He makes walking among the flower gardens or learning how to fish fun." She filled Grandfather in on her adventure.

"How can I care so much after a few short weeks?"

"Often, when you find your soul mate, time isn't an issue. You were raised in New Mexico, but it doesn't mean you have to stay here all your life." He picked up the pictures. "Seems you're at a cross-road. Do you let love slip away, or, throw caution aside and give happiness a chance?" Take serious thought to your situation with Trace."

"None of this matters anyway." Father would never support my relationship."

"Your Father wouldn't encourage any situation which doesn't fit into his window of perfection." Since you've been grown, how many times have your father's notions hindered you? You've bucked the monarch of the Willis family before. I love you and want your happiness, no matter what."

She went to her grandfather, bent down and hugged him. "I love you, too. I'll consider our conversation. For now, I'm going to see if the wine is ready for you to sample."

After taking Grandfather a glass of wine, Barbary quietly closed his bedroom door and stepped into the hallway. She removed the photo of her and Trace from her pocket and ran her finger over his face. The conversation about letting happiness pass

by nagged at her. She slipped the photo into her
pocket and headed down the hallway.

Barbary stared at the digital clock. Well beyond the midnight hour, the silence in the house
seemed overwhelming. She grabbed her robe and
made the way downstairs to get a glass of juice.
Barbary trotted back to her room and booted
her laptop. The screen brightened, and a ding
sounded, indicating a new message.
She scanned the emails and clicked a link to a
social site from one of her friends. She read the subject line, "country club party Saturday," and leaned
back considering the invitation. "I do need to get
back to normal."
The next email announced career opportunities. Barbary opened the form letter listing a need
for Graphic Designers in various states. She looked
over the list, scrolled to an opening for an intern
with an advertisement agency in New York and followed the page to the application. She bookmarked
the prospect and moved to the next prospect.
Barbary eyed the listing while she took a drink
of juice. A position from North Carolina made her
hand shake. She quickly set her glass down, then
gasped when the glass tilted on the edge of the desk
and spilled onto the floor.
"Oh no!" She jumped up and went to her
bathroom to grab a towel.

~ * ~

On Saturday evening Barbary dressed for the
party at the country club. She added the owl necklace to her maroon dress, admired the way the silver
wings shined against the dark red material and slid
her stocking feet into a pair of four-inch heels. Her

cell rang. Without paying attention to the call log, she answered, "Hi."

"Hello." An alluring southern accent met her ear.

"Trace?"

"Please, don't be mad at me for calling. I know what you said, I only wanted to hear your voice. I promise not to pressure you into anything."

"Trace." She sat on the edge of a chair and swiped her hair from her face, while her stomach played tag with her heart. "How are you?"

"Good, I guess. We've finished the pond and the fish arrive tomorrow."

"I'm sure the spot will be pretty." She crossed her legs and eyed her gold shoe.

"Barbary, I miss you."

"I enjoy hearing your voice, too." She cradled the phone with both hands.

"I'm glad." He paused. "Please, call me sometime so we can at least talk."

"Yes." She took a breath and shook her head at the way the word tumbled from her lips without question. "Grandfather appreciates the pictures. He says you're a nice-looking young man."

"There's another reason to like him." He chuckled.

Barbary tried to keep her mind on the conversation, and not her desire to feel his arms around her. "I told Grandfather about my fishing lesson."

"You should be proud of your first attempt at being an angler. Some people try many times before they are successful."

"I didn't get my catch."

"You still hooked one."

Fifteen minutes passed while they chatted. Barbary went to her closet, retrieved her small evening bag, and slid her credit card inside. "I need to say goodbye. Leslie is picking me up in a few minutes."

He lowered his tone. "I hope Leslie is a woman."

"I assure you, she is. We're going, uh, shopping." For a reason she couldn't fathom, she didn't want to tell him about the party.

"Bye beautiful, I miss you."

"Good night." She ended the call and hung her head. *I miss you, too.*

Minutes slipped by while she replayed the conversation. Talking with Trace seemed useless. Too many miles stood between them, and phone friends were out of the question. The notion of him sharing details about a date with another woman made her frown.

She let out a breath and headed downstairs and.
entered the library. Her father shoved his phone in his pocket.

"Arrogant woman." He ran his hand through his graying hair. "Regina will be the death of me. She expects me to submit a request for a new metal analyzer. I've never jumped through hoops before to get equipment. How does she think we can break down the chemicals for our necessary evaluations?"

Barbary stifled a smile. "I think she likes you."

Her father eyed her. "She's an impossible person. Why would you think such a thing?"

"I don't know. I'm assuming if she didn't care, she would dismiss you without a word. The way you do with people you dislike. I believe she sparks something in you, too."

"Of all the nonsense. Where is your common sense? I've no desire to get involved with an emotional woman."

Barbary couldn't stifle her laugh. "I believe she intrigues you."

"I think not." He turned away for a second, then looked back at her. "Speaking of interest, what did you do in North Carolina?" He pointed toward his desk.

Barbary walked over and looked on top of a book. "Where did you get this?" She picked up the photo of her and Trace.

"In the hallway, on the floor." His eyes narrowed. "Who is sitting beside you?"

"His name is Trace. He's the managing horticulturist at Bellmore Estates."

"Imagine my shock to see a picture of you and a dark-skinned man. Now, I discover he's a gardener?" He scowled.

"Trace is not a gardener. He went to college and studied to do what he enjoys. And for your information, his heritage is Indian."

"Listen to yourself!" He barked. "Taking up with a grounds keeper."

Barbary felt her face grow hot. "His creations offer people a chance to see the beauty around the acreage."

"An hourly worker. Thank goodness you came back when you did. No telling what would have happened if you'd stayed."

"I'm not discussing this with you." Barbary gaped at her father. "I have a party at the country club to attend." She turned and left.

She paced the circle driveway and massaged her temples. An anvil colliding with her head would be better than the quarrel with her father. She exhaled. He would never change. An approaching vehicle made her stop. Her friend's two-seater sports car pulled to the curb. Barbary turned and hustled toward the vehicle. "Let's go."

Leslie pushed on the gas. "Okay. Why are you so mad?"

"Father. Sometimes, he's a poor excuse of a person."

"I don't believe he's ever angered you this way. You act like you could go to battle any minute."

Barbary leaned against the headrest, closed her eyes and focused on the sounds coming from the car engine..

"This is a good parking spot. I think we're early." Leslie put her keys in her purse.

"I can take the time to get my good mood back." Barbary attempted a grin.

"We can stroll to the gazebo and admire the little blooms on the Blue Mist plants while we wait."

"Wonderful idea, Leslie."

They made their way to the side of the country club. Several benches invited members to relax. Barbary took a seat. "This is nice."

"It's a wonder how gardeners get the flowers to stay pretty." Leslie crossed her ankles.

"Many of them go to college to learn horticulture." Barbary watched the dark blue blossoms sway in the breeze.

"Hmm." Leslie shrugged. "I those guys automatically knew how to cultivate plants."

Barbary turned to her friend and frowned. Somehow, the vacation to North Carolina matured her. Now she couldn't understand how Leslie dismissed everything. "Leslie, situations aren't always one sided."

"I guess not." Leslie leaned closer to Barbary. "Pretty necklace."

"This is an original from a craft store in Asheville."

"Really?" Her friend picked up the necklace, gazed at the emerald eyes and let it fall back onto Barbary's dress collar. "I started to ask about the trip, but you seemed too upset."

"The mountains held an adventure." One I'll never get over."

"Do tell." Leslie straightened a ring on her finger. "Somewhere in the south, right?"

"Asheville. You want to hear about my vacation in the mountains?"

"I'm sure the trip won't live up to Paris but tell me anyway."

"The Bellmore Estates is a magnificent place. The mountain area is breathtaking." Barbary painted a mental image of the estate, the winery, and the shopping areas in downtown Asheville. "There are a lot of beautiful flowers and shrubbery on the grounds it takes a lot of hard work to keep plants growing pretty."

"Huh?" Leslie glanced at Barbary. "How would you know?" She laughed. "Never mind."

"Leslie, we've known each other a long time."

"Sure, since sixth grade. You befriended me when our family moved here for Dad's new job at the lab."

"I remember how difficult those first months were before you adjusted. Going to Asheville gave me a reason to want to make some changes too."

"You're talking strange." Leslie glanced at the parking spots that were filling. "Better explain fast. The fun is starting."

Barbary stood. "We should attend the party."

They walked through the double doors and made their way to the bar. The bartender handed them a glass of wine. Barbary smiled and mouthed, "Thanks."

"Oh look, there's Patrick." Leslie nodded toward the other side on the room.

"You should join him."

"Are you sure? I don't want to leave you here alone, especially if you're still feeling down."

Barbary laughed lightly. "I'm fine, go, I'm going to mingle."

With the passing hour, the crowd doubled, and a man sauntered her way.

"Barbary. Good to see you. Where have you been?"

"Vacation, remember?" She stood rigid when he kissed her cheek.

"Some little nowhere place, I recall." He frowned.

"North Carolina." She eyed Lance, noticing the harshness of his face. Not at all like Trace's caring disposition.

He took her arm. "Oh, well. Let's forget your futile trip and enjoy a quiet time on my yacht." He leaned near and mumbled. "The two of us."

She jerked away. "I think not."

"What? You're turning me away? There are women who would be grateful to spend time with me."

Barbary eyed him. His condescending tone reminded her of Father. She gritted her teeth. "I suggest from now on that you find one of those women."

"I can't believe you've spoken to me in such a fashion. One day you'll regret this decision." He turned on his heels and hurried off.

She took a swallow from her goblet and headed to the bar. "Would you like more wine?" The bartender smiled. "I believe you've nursed the one glass since you've been here."

"Actually, I want a mineral water." She set the flute on the bar.

"Coming right up."

Barbary scanned the room and found Leslie huddled with Patrick. She watched her friend and reminisced about being in Trace's arms. The server loudly cleared his throat.

"You're miles away." He placed a tumbler in front of her.

"Guess so." She moved the water and the ice danced around.

"Troubled? I'm a good listener." He wiped the counter.

Red, green, and white wavy lines flash from a neon sign behind the bartender. She smiled half-heartedly. "Circumstances can take a turn sometimes."

Eleven

*B*arbary's attention strayed from the blinking colors behind the counter to the bartender.

"People can't change the life they're born into. Talking won't help."

"You never can tell." He shrugged. "What's inspired you to want things to be different? I've seen you in here many times. You seem carefree and happy."

"I guess, before I opened my eyes to other possibilities." She stared at her manicured nails. "You don't have time to listen to my despair."

"Maybe I want to."

"Have you always been a bartender?"

"Yeah. I enjoy mixing drinks and experimenting with flavors is fun."

Barbary laughed. "You remind me of someone I met recently."

"You mentioned a person can't change the way they were born. I think they can. Do you mind a short story?"

"Not at all." Barbary watched the dimple on his cheek deepen when he smiled.

"Let's say a man is born within a family of doctors. Of course, everyone expects him to become a medical professional. In his last months of high school, he decides not to become a doctor. Now, he makes a living helping people enjoy their hobbies and teaches golf. He's content and productive, despite what the rest of his family thinks."

"And you told me this because?" She tapped her fingers on the granite counter.

"I'm only saying people can change, if they desire. My dad is from a family of neurosurgeons. He's never liked the sight of blood and chose to live on his own terms, so I know you don't have to stay in the mold your family sets." His eyes crinkled at the corners. "I should get back to mixing drinks, customers are waiting."

"Thanks for the story."

Leslie stepped up to the bar "Talking to the bartender?" She frowned. "You didn't leave with Lance."

"The bartender is nice, but Lance? I'm finished with him forever."

"Wow, you are in a mood." Leslie quickly finished her drink and set her glass down. "I'm going to Patrick's townhouse. Do you want to drive my car home?" She held out the keys.

"No, I'll call my driver."

"Are you sure?" Leslie put her keys back in her purse.

"Positive. Go, enjoy yourself." Barbary waved her hand in the air. "We'll talk later."

"Okay." Leslie hurried away.

Twenty-five minutes later Barbary stood under the covering of the country club entrance and watched the rain fall. The family car approached, and she rushed inside.

"Hector, thanks for coming."

"Not a problem, Ms. Barbary." The driver steered onto the main road.

Barbary stared out the window, watching rain droplets cascade down the glass. One after another, beads of water followed a straight path, with only a scant few venturing sideways. She recalled the story the bartender told and tried to decide which bead of water she wanted to be.

~ * ~

The next morning a knock echoed through the room. Barbary sat up in bed, rubbed her eyes and called out. "Yes."

"Mia here. I have something for you."

"Just a minute."

Barbary greeted the cook and leaned against the doorframe yawning.

"Are you sick? You don't look well.

"I didn't sleep much last night. I believe I'll stay in my room most of the day. If you don't mind, bring me some brunch in a couple of hours." She offered Mia a seat. "I'll be right back."

Barbary went into her bathroom, splashed water on her face, came back into the bedroom and took a seat on the edge of the bed. "Ever since I returned from Asheville, I haven't been able to get back into the swing of things." She ran one hand through her short hair. "I went with Leslie to the country club, hoping the party would inspire me, but I called Hector to pick me up early. Perhaps, after I find a job, I'll feel more settled."

"You left the festivity early?" Mia opened the package she brought. "Out of character for you."

"I know. Being in Asheville, around all the nature, changed me somehow."

"The scenery, or the nice gentleman you told me about?"

Barbary sighed and looked across the room. "Occasionally, Trace is on my mind."

"Barbary, do you believe the young man in Asheville feels the same way?"

"He does."

84

"I see." Mia took a book out of the bag. "You have some important thinking to do."

"Why? People go through these situations all the time. They meet each other and, for reasons unknown, never get together."

"I guess." Smart folks realize a chance for true love." She handed Barbary a Bible. "Anyway, I wanted to bring this to you. Your mother's Bible. She wanted you to have it at the right time. I think now is good."

Barbary opened the Holy Word. She took an uneven breath and gazed at her mother's handwriting. Her name written across the dedication page, along with Barbary's birthday. On the margin a verse, *'Start children off on the way they should go, and even when they are old they will not turn from it.'* Proverbs 22:6 was printed in capital letters. She glanced at Mia and whispered, "Thank you."

"You're welcome." Mia stood and went to the door. "You'll find some of your mother's favorite scriptures highlighted. Your mom wanted you to experience the same faith she relied on." The cook stepped into the hall and closed the door. Barbary held the Bible and mumbled, "Mother, I remember you taking me to Sunday school." She flipped the pages and stopped on a highlighted verse in Hebrews, *'Now faith is confidence in what we hope for and assurance about what we do not see.'* She closed the book and mulled over the meaning.

Two hours passed. Barbary freshened-up and finished blow-drying her hair. When she went back into her room, she spotted a tray the cook left.

Barbary lifted the lid to find a blueberry muffin, coffee, juice, and a bowl filled with berries and melons. She grinned and popped a strawberry into her mouth. "Thanks Mia."

She picked up the fruit and turned on her laptop, armed with the determination to update her resume and fill out a few more applications.

The late-afternoon sun streaked across the room. Barbary smiled, and bit down on the pen she used to jot reference numbers while she looked over job opportunities. The idea of maintaining a website, creating content for the Internet, and submitting ideas for print publications appealed.. She clicked send, leaned back in the chair and studied the name of the familiar city. *What are the odds of finding a job opening in Asheville?*

~ * ~

The following evening Barbary picked up Grandfather's birthday gift and card. She eyed the Bellmore logo lavishly displayed on the front. Her mind traveled to North Carolina and the man who, in a matter of weeks turned her life upside down.

She ambled down the stairs to find her father standing beside a friend, while music played low, filling the room. Grandfather sat in his wheelchair next to the sectional sofa with a dozen other guests gathered close.

Barbary made her way to Grandfather. "Happy birthday." She kissed his cheek.

"Thank you." Grandfather addressed a man standing near, "You remember Barbary? She's the best granddaughter anyone could ask for."

"Yes." The older man hovered closer. "Young lady, I haven't seen you in years." He shook her hand. "You're all grown-up."

"I suppose." Barbary nodded at the balding man. "Excuse me. I need to speak to Father." She grinned at Grandfather and crossed the room to where her father stood, talking with a friend. When the conversation slowed, she said, "This is a nice gathering."

"Yes." Her father's friend answered. "You look lovely today."

"Thank you. Are you and Father catching up on the golf scores?"

"No use, Joe's game is never up to par." Father chuckled at his own joke.

"Barbary, much as it pains me to say, your father is right. I'll never be the player he is."

"I'm sure you give Father a run for his money." Barbary reached for a cup of punch. "Please, excuse me."

She turned and went to the crowd gartered around Grandfather, who examined his new audio reader.

"I'm sure my granddaughter will help me figure out how to work this."

Barbary nodded. "Of course, I will."

She stayed among the circle of friends who surrounded her older relative while he opened gifts. Grandfather tore into the package Barbary handed him. He marveled at a lap blanket with a mountain scene. His name embellished on a snow peak. "Barbary, thank you." Grandfather glanced at one of his friends. "She recently went to my favorite place in the states and brought back lots of wonderful mementos for my collection."

Minutes later, Barbary slipped from the gathering and made her way upstairs. Once she changed into her lounge clothes, she pressed a familiar number. Hopefully, the answering message would play. All she wanted was to hear Trace's voice, then she'd be content.

Twelve

*B*arbary exhaled, residing herself to the fact Trace left a mark on her heart, too.

"Hello." His soothing tone crossed the miles and comforted her like the gentle scent of the flowers back in North Carolina.

"Hi," she whispered.

"God answers prayers," he replied.

"What?" She held the phone tight, wishing she could reach out and touch him.

"I've been praying you would call."

"I see." She glanced at her mother's Bible on the table as she went out on the balcony. The stars twinkled in a cloudless sky. "I'll admit I wanted to hear your voice."

"I'm glad." He sneezed. "Excuse me. I'm think I'm coming down with a summer cold."

"Oh, dear! I hope it isn't bad."

"Only a sniffle. Of course, if you were here, you could make me feel better."

"I wish." She quickly put her hand to her mouth, not sure why she'd said those words aloud.

"Barbary, I know North Carolina isn't New Mexico. If you could have a life here, I'd do anything in my power to make you happy. I believe we'd find we're meant to spend our lives together."

"My." *Our lives.* Barbary licked her lips and weighed the meaning of his words. "Since I came back home, I've discovered many things about myself and some are a little confusing. I need time."

"If you want to bend an ear, I'm here." He lowered his voice. "I'll be long suffering."

"Long suffering?" She walked back inside, sat down and wiggled her toes, eyeing her pedicure.

"The term is usually found in the Bible and refers to bearing situations for a long time, without being bitter. The Lord is longsuffering towards us, not wanting any of us to perish without accepting salvation." He paused. "I'm trying to say I'll wait on you. Will you think about us?"

"Yes." She slumped from the significance of her admission. "I'm sorry, I'm suddenly tired. I like chatting with you."

"Call again soon."

She tossed the phone on the bed and frowned. A simple conversation turned her emotions upside down.

Barbary went to her desk and retrieved the Bible. She fingered the worn spine, opened the book, flipped to the back and searched the concordance for verses with the word *longsuffering*. After reading several passages, she held the Bible to her chest. A vague memory of being with her Mother in church made her smile.

~ * ~

The early morning light filled the room. Barbary turned toward the rosy glow coming through the window. After a few minutes, she got out of the bed, picked an outfit for the day and showered. Later, Barbary pushed her curtains back to brighten the room, took a seat, and turned on her laptop. The electronic mail indicator chime.

Barbary clicked on a correspondence from a production agency and leaned in to the monitor. *Your application meets our requirements. Please call to schedule an in-depth interview concerning the position of assistant designer in our New York video department.* She rubbed the polish on her nail and debated living in New York.

Barbary printed off the information and scanned the last memo. "I can't believe this!"

She read an invitation to call for a preliminary interview in North Carolina. "Produce graphics and visual representation of our tourist facility in the form of paper and Internet ads. Better than creating videos." The copier hummed again while she printed off contact information.

Downstairs, Barbary headed to the dining room. Her father turned when she entered. "I wondered if you were coming to join Grandfather and me for breakfast."

She offered an apologetic look. "I lost track of time answering emails."

"I'm sure your socialite friends can wait to enlighten you on the latest gossip." Father's frown sized her up.

"For your information I received several replies concerning my job search. I've filled out online applications." She waited for Mia to place croissants on the table. "I actually have two promising offers. One's in New York."

"Would you move there?" Grandfather reached for the butter.

"I suppose." Barbary smiled. "I've applied for positions in New Mexico, so far, no response."

"New York can offer a decent life, providing you choose a prosperous city." Father's cell phone buzzed. He glanced at the screen. "The office. I need to take this." He rose from the table to take his call in the next room.

Barbary spooned a serving of eggs. "Grandfather, I'm glad you joined us this morning."

"I believe this new medicine the doctor prescribed is helping. I feel better today." He puffed out his chest with a show of strength. "So, what do you think about this job offer?"

"I don't know." She put her fork down. "To tell you the truth, I've never considered New York." She lowered her voice. "I also received a job offer in North Carolina."

"Close to the mountains?" Grandfather looked cheerful.

"You'd approve."

Commotion from the other room made her glance toward her Father. He paused in the doorway and bellowed, "I must go to the office."

Barbary glanced at Grandfather. "The smallest situation seems to displease him."

"Indeed. A wonder he doesn't have high blood pressure." Grandfather wheeled from his spot at the table to sit next to Barbary. "Whatever decision you make concerning your career, I'll support you."

"Thanks, I may make a phone call to find out more about the opportunity in North Carolina."

~ * ~

Barbary studied the paper on her desk. The job offer in North Carolina seemed too good to be true. On impulse, she pressed Trace's number.

"Hello?"

"Hold..." His comment crackled over the airwaves. "Wait..." A half-second later, his voice was clear. "I'm sorry. I wasn't getting a good signal. I'm happy you called."

"Are you busy?" She pictured his smile and silky black hair.

"I'll always make time to chat with you."

"You're sweet. Is the pond completed?"

"I wish you could see the fish swimming around."

"A peaceful place, I'm sure." She glanced at the address of the company needing an ad designer.

"The facility manager at the gardens told me she expects a big draw of sightseers."

"Trace, do you have any knowledge about the business side of Bellmore Estates?"

"You mean the offices?"

"Yes. Does a professional staff oversee the everyday events?"

"When you work on the grounds you don't pay much attention." He laughed. "There is an office building tucked away from the estate grounds. Pay-roll is processed there. Why?"

"Being inquisitive about how a big tourist at-traction keeps going." Are you almost finished with your work day?"

"I won't be here much longer. Mom and I are going to Bible study later. Usually, I pick her up for dinner and we go to church."

"Your mother is a lucky woman."

"No, I'm a fortunate son. After Dad died, Mom worked hard to make sure I received a good educa-tion. She wanted me to be a dentist." He chuckled. "Can you picture me pulling teeth?"

"You're a handsome man." I can imagine women faking toothaches to come to your office."

"I don't know but I'd be happy to pretend to be your doctor."

"My." She briefly fanned her face at the sur-prising turn in the conversation. "We should change the subject."

Trace chuckled. "Yeah, your call made my day. The only thing better would be to hold you in my arms."

She sighed. "I'm thinking about what you said, I should hang-up now. Bye Trace." Barbary ended the call and eyed the phone. "I miss you."

Bits of their conversation replayed, along with scenarios between her and Trace and possibilities of any future together. *Regrets and decisions.* Her situation with Trace required more thought than the normal problems she encountered.

~ * ~

The pitter-patter of rain landed on the window. Barbary glared at the chilly, gray morning. A bad storm hammered the yard and thunder echoed throughout the rooms. She shivered, grabbed a long sleeve shirt and trotted downstairs. Her father sipped coffee.

"Good morning, Father."

He looked at her and motioned toward the window. "I see nothing good. The rain is atrocious."

"I figured you'd be at the office by now." She poured a cup of coffee.

"Regina called and said the power is out in my building." He set his mug down. "At least, we have a generator for the main part of the plant. Perhaps, now the woman will see a need to order back-up for the corporate staff. You'd think we would be the most important."

"I'm sure you are. Still, vital work happens inside the lab. They need power."

"For once, I agree. Work in the lab must continue."

The doorbell echoed from the hallway.

"I wonder who is out in this weather." Barbary trotted to the foyer and opened the door to find a woman holding an umbrella. "May I help you?"

"This is the residence of Ronald Willis, is it not?"

"Yes,"

"I'm Regina. I work with Mister Willis."

"Come in. Father is in the library." She led the guest to the other room and added. "I'm Barbary."

"Ronald mentions you on occasion."

"We don't always agree. I'm sure you were receptive to some misguided wrath he held toward me."

Regina lightly touched Barbary's arm. "Between us women, your father is mule-headed. Still, I enjoy sparing with him, and have designs to tamper his ill temper one day."

"Really?" Barbary snickered. "He needs you in his life. He's been bitter far too long."

They reached the library, Barbary tried to hide her satisfaction when she saw the look on Father's face.

"Why are you here this morning?" He asked Regina.

"I know you dislike driving in the rain. I thought I'd give you a lift to Nukerson."

"A lift?" He raised a brow. "You talk like I'm some kind of machine."

"Gibberish. If you were a machine, I could shut you up sometimes." Regina grinned. "Come on, let's go. You don't want to be late for your meeting."

"Go on, ride with her. She won't bite." Barbary covered her mouth to hide amusement.

"Women." He turned on his heels and picked up his briefcase. "Having females around creates a never-ending carnival."

"My car is waiting," Regina yelled over her shoulder on the way to the door.

Barbary's laughter filled the air.

94

"Your happiness is a good change from the storm." Mia replaced the coffee decanter.

"I met Regina. I like her."

"So, where are they?"

"Regina is driving Father to work."

"There is an old saying, if only I were a fly on the wall, or in this case, in the car." The cook laughed. "I'm sure their conversation would be entertaining."

"Indeed." Barbary nodded. "Did I mention I received two emails with career possibilities?"

"No. What are you going to do?"

Thirteen

A clap of thunder boomed and Barbary paused for a second to let it pass. "I need to call both companies. I hope when I speak with someone in administration I'll have a better focus on each job."

"You should choose the one that sparks your creative juices." "Are they near here?"

"I haven't received any response from the ones in New Mexico. I applied in Santa Fe and Albuquerque but didn't even get a thank-you." The responses I've received are from New York and North Carolina."

"I've been praying the Lord will guide your footsteps. Perhaps, He is."

"Mia, I can understand God helping you. I doubt the Lord will direct me. I'm sure I'm not living how He wishes."

"Barbary, I'm not perfect. I try each day and sometimes I fall short. Still, I can tell you God answers prayers. If I pray for you, I believe He honors my prayers. I must go and start the dishwasher."

Barbary went upstairs to Grandfather's room. She knocked on the door.

"Come in."

She stepped inside to find him in bed. "Grandfather, is everything all right?" She went to a chair next to his bed.

"Today is not good, I'm feeling tired." He attempted to grin. "I'm getting old Barbary."

Despite his pale complexion, she plastered a smile on her face. "You're still filled with energy."

"Child, there is something you need to know."
He flinched. "The doctor says my old ticker is worn
out. I'm afraid I don't have many days left with my
family."

Barbary held her breath. His words seared her
heart. She willed threatening tears back. "Isn't
there something they can do, an operation?"

"No. Doc says I wouldn't be a good candidate
for heart surgery." He grasped her hand. "My legacy
will live on in you. I want you to conquer your part
of the world for me. Make me proud."

The burn in Barbary's throat threatened to
bring forth a well of tears. She swallowed hard. "I
love you." She leaned over him and kissed his cheek.

"I love you, too." Now, I must rest."

"Of course, I'll come back later." She walked
to his door and looked over her shoulder. "Is there
anything I can get you?"

"Yes. Some wine you brought back from North
Carolina would be good."

"Mia will bring you a glass after dinner."

The realization of her grandfather's immortal-
ity choked her. She rushed to her room and threw
herself on the bed. The blanket soon became damp
from hushed tears.

The hours passed without Barbary noticing
she'd missed dinner. She washed her face and hurried downstairs to the kitchen to find the cook.

"Mia, Grandfather wants a glass of Bellmore's
wine."

"Very well. Your eyes are puffy. Is everything
all right?"

"Grandfather told me he's ill."

"Aha, I wondered when he planned to tell
you."

"You knew? Why didn't you tell me?"

"Your grandfather said he would, when the right time came."

Barbary looked at the floor. "This changes thins. I can't entertain the idea of moving when his health is bad."

"Haven't you been listening to your grandfather?" His desire is for you to be productive and happy. The place isn't important. Sometimes, the right opportunities only come by once."

"I can't think about a career right now." Barbary let out a breath. "Does Father know?"

"Of course, but he wanted your grandfather to tell you."

"I see. Where is Father?"

The cook poured her cake batter into a Bundt pan. "He left a message he'd be late. Regina talked him into going to the country club for dinner."

Barbary smiled. "At least, something good is happening. I'll take Grandfather's drink. Please, prepare me a hoagie with a glass of milk for later."

She left with the tray and made her way upstairs. "Grandfather?"

"Yes." His voice sounded sluggish. "Come in."

"I brought your wine." She set the tray down and handed him the goblet.

"Wonderful." He lifted the glass to his nose, inhaled and took a sip. "Ah, this is good. Sit for a while."

Barbary took a seat and waited while grandfather enjoyed his drink.

"Aren't you joining me?"

"I may sample a glass before I go to bed." She pressed her lips tight. The way Grandfather savored the beverage she'd keep every ounce for him.

He took another drink and held the bottom of the goblet with both hands. "Did you call about those jobs?"

"No." She shook her head.

"You should, before the positions are filled."

"I don't want to leave home right now."

"Listen," Grandfather's wobbly voice stern. "I'd like to know you're in a fulfilling position, even if relocation is necessary." "Don't pass this up. This is the first time since you graduated that you've been interested in beginning a career."

Barbary looked at Grandfather. Words drained him. He put his hand on his chest. The many times before, where he'd spoken to her about settling down plagued her thoughts. "I understand the importance for me to," she made air quotes, "find my place in the world."

"Please, don't make light of my wishes. I'm older, and hopefully, wiser. I happen to know contributing to society builds ones' self-worth. You may have money, but self-esteem is something which comes from integrity."

"You remind me of Trace. I can hear him saying the same thing."

"I think the young man has a lot going for him. You've always been quick to give up. You shouldn't take Trace for granted."

"Father would be furious if anything serious happened between us."

"Probably. Are you going to let him dictate your life?"

"No." She stood and leaned over to kiss her grandfather's almost bald head. "I'll let you rest."

"Don't dismiss our chat."

Barbary returned the glass to the kitchen, sat at the table, and bit into her sandwich, barely tasting the ham and turkey. With each chew, Grandfather's discussion replayed in her mind.

Later, she headed back to her room. Night became morning with her grandfather's words drifting through her dreams.

~ * ~

Barbary quickly opened her eyes and glanced at the digital clock. If she hurried, she could see her father before he left for work. "I wonder how he enjoyed Regina's presence at dinner."

Fifteen minutes later Barbary bounded downstairs to the dining room. "Good Morning Father." She took a seat. "I missed you last night at dinner."

"Really?" Father raised one brow.

"I normally find you in the library, or in your office." She tried to keep a straight face, so he wouldn't pick up on her curiosity.

"Daughter, don't play coy. You obviously have something on your mind."

Barbary watched the cook place biscuits on the table. "Mia, this is wonderful. I can't recall the last time we enjoyed homemade biscuits."

"Grandfather requested them. I can't bake one without making a whole pan."

"I'm glad." Barbary took a biscuit and reached for the butter. "Grandfather told me about his health."

"Should have months ago. He's been going downhill for a while. Now, you know why he takes most of his meals in his room. He tires easily."

"I came to speak with you, after I found out. Mia said you were at the country club."

"Regina is so irritating. She refused to bring me home until I went to dinner."

Barbary chewed, determined not to let him see the smile dancing around her mouth. "I'm sure she means well. Perhaps Regina needed company. We did have showers all day. Sometimes rain tends to make people sad."

"Humph. I have to admit I'm quite surprised, being around her isn't unpleasant."

Barbary had to force herself not to smile. "You know, being in someone else's company once in a while is nice."

"I suppose."

"Father, may I discuss something with you?"

"Of course." He looked at her.

"When I spoke with Grandfather last night he mentioned his wish is for me to begin my career. So, I'm going to make phone calls today and see where they lead."

"Grandfather's desire is for you to utilize your degree." He spoke in a softer tone. "The main reason I wanted you to get the internship at the laboratory is because my career, along with your grandmother and mother's influences are there. We're all part of the laboratory. I figured the place would also suit you."

"I'll be happier working where I can create more than charts and statistical graphs." She rested her chin on her hand. Barbary glanced at her father. For the first time in years, she caught a glimpse of compassion. "I miss Mother and I want everyone to be proud of me but being part of the lab will only make me miserable."

"Very well. You're determined. One thing I've learned about women is when they decide on something, it's like a puppy with a toy, they won't give up." Crow's feet formed with the tiniest grin.

"Thank you." Barbary rose from her seat and hugged him. "Maybe Regina is mellowing you."

"She may be the death of me yet." He picked up his coat. "Still, someone should keep an eye on her, for the sake of the laboratory."

"I agree." She turned and smiled as her father left. Barbary chuckled. He seemed pleasant this morning. Regina must have a positive influence on him. She headed to her room.

~ * ~

The laptop woke when she touched the pad. She scanned messages and deleted several on-line shopping coupons.

A memo from the company in North Carolina grabbed her attention. She clicked the message box. *Dear Miss Barbary Willis, we haven't received a call about our available position. If you're sincere about this opening the deadline to apply is in two weeks.* She pushed against the chair and her cell chimed.

"Hello."

"Barbary, hopefully, I didn't wake you," Trace's voice crossed the airwaves.

"No, I've been up for a while."

"Do you have any fun plans today?"

Barbary heard the birds chirping in the background and pictured Trace standing on the grounds at Bellmore. "I'm planning to spend time with Grandfather. I remember when I was younger, we played checkers. I believe the board is still in my closet."

"I'm sure your grandfather will enjoy a game. How are things with your Father?"

"Father's fine. We actually carried on a nice conversation at breakfast."

"Good."

"Trace, I'm glad you called. I found out Grandfather is very sick." Her voice broke. "He says there's nothing the doctors can do."

"I'm sorry. I'll be sure to remember you both in prayer."

"Thanks. I need to go. I have something important to do before I let Grandfather beat me in checkers."

"Work waits for me too. I'll talk to you later, beautiful."

She laid the phone down and picked up the contact information she'd printed earlier. One of these positions could define the rest of her life. Ten minutes into a phone call, she ambled to the window and rolled her eyes toward the clouds while she listened to the manager from the video company in New York describe the position. *Games.* Her chest rose with indecision.

"There's not much more I can tell you over the phone. We are conducting interviews on Wednesdays and Fridays. When can we schedule you a time?"

"I need to check my calendar." Barbary held the phone between her shoulder and her chin.

"Today will be good to tighten your agenda. Our interview spots fill quickly."

"All right, I have your contact number. Thank you." She put the phone down and focused on the idea of creating backgrounds for video games.

Barbary went to her desk and made a call to the other company. Several transfers later, she spoke to an advertising executive. The woman highlighted a need for someone to be in tune to the different ways to take advantage of marketing for travelers and tourists.

"We are an old establishment and could use young blood to bring a fresh approach to marketing. We strive to stay ahead of progress and challenge our employees to find innovative ways to be creative. I have an opening next week. I'll book you for the comprehensive interview on Thursday. Can you be here at four?"

Without thought, Barbary said, "I can."

"Wonderful. I'll email directions."

Barbary held onto the phone long after the conversation ended. Everything had happened so fast. *I can always cancel.* She gathered her checker set and took off to Grandfather's room.

Fourteen

" *C*ome in," Grandfather said.

Barbary stepped into his room. "Do you remember when we used to play checkers?" She held out the game.

"I do." He wheeled over to the table. "Do you think you can beat your old Grandfather?"

"I'm not twelve anymore, I'm smarter." She set up the checker set. "You use the black checkers and I'll let you go first."

"So, you're feeling confident?" He moved his disc and grinned. For ten minutes, they concentrated on the checkerboard.

"Grandfather, you didn't!" She shook her head when he captured her red disc.

"Child, I played the game with your mother." He laughed lightly. "You remind me of her, always optimistic about winning." He took another turn. "Crowned."

"I haven't played in years. I'm rusty."

He touched a checker and glanced at Barbary. "Have you made any decisions about your career?"

"I called the two connections I've made." She captured his black checker and grinned. "I don't know about the one in the New York."

"I remember spending some time there in my younger years. I wasn't too impressed." He crowned another disc. "Course, I like open spaces."

"I also talked to the executive of a vacation destination. They need someone to create impressive ads to draw in the tourists."

"The one in North Carolina?" Grandfather rubbed his chin.

"Actually, I have an interview scheduled for next week. Things happened fast."

"Go. Some of the best decisions are made at the spur of the moment. Where in North Carolina, is this place located?"

Barbary captured one of Grandfather's checkers. "Bellmore Estates."

"Hot dog!" Grandfather wheezed. "I think the stars are guiding you."

"Stars? I imagine Trace would say the Lord leads us."

"Is Trace a religious young man?"

"Yes, his mother raised him to revere God." She grinned at his last move. "I can't believe you beat me."

"Granddaughter, I'm still a winner."

"You'll always be a winner in my eyes." Barbary gently patted his wrinkled hand resting on the table. "Are you ready for another game?" She gathered the checkers.

"Your mother was a fine Christian woman."

"She took me to church. I'd forgotten about those Sundays until Mia gave me Mother's Bible."

"She always treated her Bible like a precious stone and talked to me about Jesus." He took a hard breath. "When my daughter got too sick to quote a Bible verse, I knew the Leukemia had taken its toll."

"Trace would say she's in heaven."

"Your mother always assured me she'd be in a better place. Can you imagine? She comforted me in her sickness."

"She loved everyone."

"Indeed. Maybe, I should have listened to her better. They say Christians know each other in heaven. I sure would like to see her again."

Barbary contemplated his words. "I wish I knew how to help. Next time, I speak with Trace I'll try to remember to ask."

"He really does sound like a good man." Grandfather moved a checker. Are you going to interview at Bellmore?"

Barbary glanced at her grandfather. For the first time in days, she noticed happiness on his face. She sat up straight, determined to keep the smile shining. "I dread telling Father."

"Stand your ground child. Do this and say hello your young man."

"Do you think I should?" Barbary mulled over his words. *My young man.*

Grandfather's voice brought her back to the game. "Don't toss away a chance for happiness."

"I'll take your wisdom into consideration." She removed his black checker and nodded. "And I may win this game."

"So you say." Grandfather studied the board.

An hour later, Barbary noticed her grandfather's slumped posture. "These games seem to tire me out," she said.

"I should lie down and rest, too." He wheeled from the table to his bed.

"I'll help you get settled."

"Thanks, I can usually get myself to bed, but you've worn me out."

She helped him settle on his bed, and said, "I'll come back later."

"I've enjoyed our game." Grandfather closed his eyes. "Maybe, next time you'll win."

She laughed and kissed his cheek. "Rest well."

Barbary went back to her room, reached for her phone pressed the screen and mentally noted the time difference between New Mexico and North Carolina.

"Hello," Trace's pleasant greeting came quickly.

"Hi, did I catch you on a break?"

"The boss can take a mini-break anytime if needed." He chuckled. "I'm glad you called."

"I enjoyed several rousing games of checkers with Grandfather."

"Did he win?"

"Of course, but he gets so tired." She rubbed her head. "Despite everything, he's in good spirits."

"Barbary, sometimes all anyone can do is to make the best of their time."

"I suppose." She walked onto her terrace. "I have a job interview next week."

"An easy commute for you, I hope."

"Actually, no. If I get this position, I'll relocate." She cleared her throat. "I may have a chance to stop by Bellmore before I fly back home."

"Please, come by. I miss you. Tell me more about your opportunity."

"Not yet." Barbary bit her cheek. "I have to go. I have things to do."

"What day next week will I see you?"

"I'll find you." She laughed and ended the call.

She slipped her phone into her pocket, held on to the railing of the balcony, and eyed the swimming pool. The glistening water beckoned. She quickly went back inside to change into her bathing suit.

Barbary swam the perimeter of the pool. A few laps later, she took her place on a lounge chair, closed her eyes and soaked in the summer rays.

"May I bring you some lemonade?" Mia asked.

"Yes." She opened her eyes. "With lots of ice."

"No problem."

Minutes passed, and then Mia's voice broke Barbary's solitude, "I haven't seen you use the pool this year." She set the tray with a pitcher, a glass and a couple of coconut cookies on the side table.

"This is the first time. I thought the scenery would help me sort out a few things. I have so much on my mind, and a conversation with Father later." She reached for a cookie. "One I'm not looking forward to."

"Oh." Mia shaded her eyes. "Care to share?"

Barbary replayed her telephone conversations with both job prospects. "The position in New York doesn't feel right, but I enjoyed speaking with the manager in Asheville. Before I realized it, I agreed to a face-to-face interview next week."

Mia picked up the empty tray. "Remember, this is your decision. Not your father's"

"I know." Barbary frowned and bite into her sweet treat.

"I've known you since you were a child, your quietness tells me there's more to the story." The cook held the tray to her side. "It's the young man in North Carolina?"

"We spent a lot of time together in Asheville. He thinks we could have a serious relationship."

"And what do you believe?"

"I've never cared for anyone the way I do him."

"If I could do things over, I'd never let my one love walk away. I faced a similar situation in my twenties. My mother hated the man and gave me grief about us dating. Even though my heart ached, I told him goodbye. Last I heard, he moved across the country and became a firefighter." Mia shook her head. "Can't do anything about spilled milk. Don't make the same mistake I did." Mia turned and left.

"Maybe, you never married because of him?" Barbary spoke softly when Mia went back inside the house.

~ * ~

"I won't be having dinner here this evening," Father said.

"You have plans?" Barbary entered the library and helped straighten his tie.

"I suppose. Regina accepted an invitation at a fund raiser, even told the couple I'd join her." He raised a brow. "What possessed the woman to say such a thing? The man is a scientist with the lab. I didn't see a way to get out of it."

"You should attend." She stepped back and took a deep breath. "I have an interview next week. The executive from one of the companies I applied for wants to talk with me in person."

"In New York?"

"North Carolina." Barbary caught his daggered scowl.

"You are determined to live in deprivation."

"Everyone in North Carolina is not poor. And for your information, I like the area."

"You would, you're like your grandfather."

"Thanks." She stood straighter and met his glower with determination. "There's nothing you can say to make me cancel my plans. I leave next week."

"You may not like the consequences of your decision."

"Excuse me." Regina stepped into the room. "The cook let me in. I hope I'm not disturbing you."

"Regina, you're always around at the most inopportune times." Mister Willis glanced at her and then back at his daughter.

Barbary smiled at the guest. "We're finished. I've heard enough of Father's dissatisfaction with my interview choices."

"Ronald does have some powerful ideas," Regina said.

"I'm glad you understand him. He's unique." Barbary crossed her arms and glanced her father's way.

"You two can stop talking like I'm not here." I'm sure the car is ready for us."

"Regina, enjoy your evening" Barbary ran up the stairs. *You may not like the consequences of your decision.* His words haunted her.

Fifteen

"*I* should leave within the half-hour," Barbary spoke with the driver from the veranda. "I have my luggage in the hallway."

"Very well. Everything will be in the car when you're ready."

She went back inside the house and trotted to Grandfather's door.

"Come in."

Barbary cracked the door and peeked inside. "I wanted to say goodbye. I'll only be away a couple days." She smiled.

"You have all your arrangements made for the trip?"

"Yes. I'm headed to the airport. My interview is this afternoon." She stooped down and kissed Grandfather's cheek. "I love you."

"I love you, too, my granddaughter. I'm pleased you're pursuing this."

"I'll call and fill you in with all the details." She took hold of his hand. "I may not be a good candidate for this position."

"Hopefully, the manager will see the potential in you I know is there." He squeezed her hand.

"I must go."

"Good luck."

~ * ~

Barbary hurried from the elevator of Bellmore Gardens, scooted inside her rental car and looked at the printed directions to the business office of Bellmore Gardens. *A couple of blocks away.* She circled around the grounds toward her destination.

An open area with an antique writing desk welcomed her. She took a quick look at an overgrown banana plant sitting to the side of the room. Pictures of the estate spanned through the years and decorated the walls. Barbary walked to the empty desk and looked around. A woman exited a door on the right and took a seat.

"I'm sorry. I stepped away for a second."

"I have an appointment to see Miss Carter."

The woman clicked on the keypad. "Barbary Willis?"

"Yes."

"I'll let her know you're here."

Barbary walked to a black and white snapshot of the estate. "Historic house museum." She glanced at the date of the picture.

"Bellmore's history is long," a woman behind her commented.

Barbary turned. The woman's blue dress, trimmed with lace caught her eye. "I'm Barbary Willis," she said with a smile.

"Miss Willis, I'm Miss Carter. You may call me Alice."

"Wonderful to meet you."

"Shall we?" Alice motioned to a door on the other side of the room. "I hope you don't mind. I have another manager sitting in for the interview."

Barbary stepped into the room. A stocky man about her father's age sat at the end of the conference table.

Alice took her place. "Have a seat."

"I see you're from New Mexico." The man gave her a wide-eyed glance. "Also, you haven't held a position since you graduated?"

"Los Alamos. I like this area very much and have a friend here. Relocation will be an easy transition."

"I see." The man laid her resume down and folded his hands on top of the paper. "Miss Willis, can you explain why you're only now pursuing an occupation in your field of study?"

"Please, be honest," Alice added, offering a smile of encouragement.

The tick-tock from the vintage-world wall clock dominated the silence. Barbary scraped her teeth over her bottom lip. Being open about her life wasn't her normal custom. "I don't have any excuses. I'm afraid I've spent the past few years undecided about a future. The time I've spent in Asheville sealed my desire to find my place in the world." She glanced at her peers. "I'm ready to dedicate myself to become the best graphic designer possible."

Alice and her colleague exchanged a quick look. The man spoke. "Miss Willis, let's say I asked you to create a new page for our latest attraction, a koi pond, what would your idea be?"

Thankfully familiar with the grounds, Barbary's confidence soared, and she straightened in the chair. "I'd highlight a few pictures of the construction process, to the now finished tranquil, fish enclosure. The important thing would be to place value on the relaxing pleasure for our visitors." She then went on to mention other design ideas. When Barbary ended her mock presentation, she hoped she'd passed their test. Alice addressed Barbary with more questions about her educational background.

Twenty minutes later, she rose from her seat. "Barbary, this meeting is encouraging."

Barbary stood, shook their hands, and followed Alice to the door.

114

"We have other interviews scheduled. I will say we're specifically searching for someone not programmed by another company. I'll contact you in a week with a decision, one way or the other."

"Thank you, I appreciate your consideration." Barbary walked away slowly, afraid she might break out into a skip. She wanted this. Her admission hit her like a rock.

~ * ~

Barbary glanced at the time and noted Trace would be home relaxing for the evening. She made her way to the parking area, backed out, and headed toward his house. Mia's words played in her mind. *Don't make the same mistake.*

The winding drive led to Trace's log home. She quietly stepped out of her car and walked to the side of the house. Trace was in a chair, leaned back with his feet propped up on a rail.

"Must be nice to have this view." She stopped suddenly when Trace jumped up and jogged toward her.

"Barbary." He picked her up, swung her around, and kissed her.

"Trace Youngbird, put me down." She laughed. "You're going to hurt your back."

He gently set her feet on the ground and kissed her with more passion.

"Wow," Barbary sighed. "I have to admit, I've missed you too."

"Since you left, I can't fill this void." He put her hand on his chest. "My heart belongs to you."

"Trace." She leaned into him, closed her eyes and soaked in the closeness she'd missed.

"Come, sit with me."

Barbary took a seat beside him. Their hands met in the middle. "This is wonderful."

"Yeah, I've never regretted my decision to build on this land." He massaged her fingers. "You didn't tell me much about the interview. I hope you didn't go too far out of the way to come by Asheville."

Barbary stared at Trace, and her smile widened. "I went to an interview at the Bellmore office."

"What? Best news all year." He let go of her hand, and scooted to the edge of his seat, facing her. "Let's take a walk and talk about the possibilities?"

"Sure." Barbary stood.

They strolled to the end of the yard, toward the pond. Barbary watched a greenish-blue dragonfly zip from one end to the other.

Trace put his arm around her shoulder. "So, tell me all about the interview."

"Nothing much to say. They're looking for a designer for marketing. Miss Carter said more applicants are scheduled."

"I'll be praying they realize you're the lady for the position."

"I'm probably up against more qualified designers."

"I know someone who can influence their decision-making process." He kissed her cheek.

"Who?"

"Jesus," Trace said with certainty. "Prayer works." He touched a strand of her hair.

"Mia says if a person is living for the Lord, He hears their petition, even for others." She eyed the ground.

"She's correct." Trace glanced at her posture. "What's wrong?"

"Thinking about Grandfather." He told me he wants to see my mother in heaven." She batted her eyes to prevent the puddle of water from spilling onto her cheek.

"If your grandfather wants forgiveness, and believes on Jesus Christ, then he can have salvation."

"Talking to you makes me feel a little better." She hugged him.

"I'll show you some Bible scriptures to guide you along the way."

Later, they sat and enjoyed iced tea. Barbary pushed her glass to the side. "I'm happy to be here with you, but I need to get back to my suite."

"I understand." He kissed her cheek. "I'll walk you to your car. Are you staying at Bellmore?"

"Yes." Trace opened the door to her rental. "I'll be here until day after tomorrow. I need to fly home back soon, Grandfather seems to grow weaker each day." She got inside and rolled down her window. "Being here with you again is wonderful."

"If you get to call Asheville home, we can always be together." He leaned closer. "Tomorrow, I'll take the day off, let me cook a nice lunch for you."

"Okay." She backed out and headed to the inn.

Sixteen

Trace watched the taillights of Barbary's rental car disappear. He moved to the sofa, took a seat and kicked off his shoes. The phone buzzed.

"Hi, Mom."

"Hello, you sound like you're in a good mood."

"I am. I saw Barbary earlier."

"I thought she went back to New Mexico."

"She came here for a job interview, at Bellmore. With God anything is possible." He cleared his throat. "When she's here, I feel complete."

"Son, you know I'll stand with you. You really do care for her, don't you?"

"I'm so close to losing my heart. We're having dinner tomorrow, before she goes back to New Mexico. Her grandfather is sick."

"Oh dear, a serious problem?"

"Not good. His heart is weak."

"I'll remember him in my prayers."

"Thanks, Mom. Rest well."

"You too, enjoy your date."

~ * ~

The fire alarm blared throughout the house. Trace jump from his lounge chair on the patio and ran inside.

"Confounded." He grabbed the oven-mitten and pulled out a black roast.

The doorbell rang. He held onto the dish and rush to greet Barbary. "Come in." He looked at the charcoal blob. "I'm sorry. I destroyed our dinner."

Barbary eyed the dark piece of meat. "Perhaps, a little over done." She giggled.

"Yeah, you think?" He joined her merriment.

Barbary stepped inside the log cabin. "So, what's for dinner now?"

"I hope you like frozen pizza. Let me get rid of this. Please, have a seat."

He came back, shaking his head. "I don't know what I did wrong. I thought I followed Mom's directions to a T."

"Accidents happen."

"At the worst time." He took a seat next to her. "I have pepperoni and cheese."

"One of my favorites." She couldn't resist the temptation to move a strand of hair off his collar.

"I'll be right back." He hurried around the counter put a pizza in the oven and poured the dinner beverages. "I remember how much you enjoyed the tea at the estate. I brought a quart home." He handed her a glass.

"Thanks." She sipped the sweet liquid and let the lemon flavor linger on her tongue a second. "Did your day go well?"

"This is the highlight of my day. And yours?" He leaned in and caressed her lips. "I enjoyed the new pond and tried to call Grandfather a few times."

"How's your grandfather?"

"Every time I called he was resting. I leave tomorrow morning at nine. I'll see him soon."

"Have you heard anything from your interview?"

Barbary glanced at him removing the pizza. "I don't expect to for another week."

He placed the meal on the island and set out two plates. Barbary joined him at the counter. "This looks good."

119

"It'll work. May I say grace? Lord, bless our food and lay you healing hand on Barbary's grandfather. Also, guide her to the career which fits into your plans." He paused, and silently petitioned, *God, if possible, make a way for her to live in Asheville.* Trace added, "Amen." He pushed the pizza dish toward her. "Ladies first." He waited for Barbary before helping himself to a serving "I'm sorry about dinner. This isn't much."

"The company is what matters."

He finished his third slice of pizza while they chatted about his work, and the marketing opportunity at Bellmore.

"I'm praying you get the graphic job."

"Wow."

"What? Why the look of concern?"

"I didn't consider all the details involved when I began searching for a position in another state. Still, I like the idea of creating advertisements for the estate. All of this seems to be happening so fast. A job opportunity and a promise for a serious relationship with you."

"I'm falling in love with you. How do you feel?"

"You're the only man I've ever missed not being around. I care for you very much."

"I assume we both would like the chance for our relationship to flourish into a commitment."

Barbary's phone chirped. She pulled the cell from the pocket of her purse, eyed the screen and read a text. "I need to call home. Father says it's urgent. He normally doesn't text."

"No reason to apologize. Go ahead and make your call." He kissed her on the cheek and went into the kitchen.

Barbary paced the floor until her father answered. "Father, is everything alright?"

"Absolutely not. I detest texting, and you wouldn't answer the cell."

"I'm sorry. Please, tell me what's wrong."

"Grandfather's health is worse. You need to fly home ASAP. This isn't good."

"I'm on the first available flight."

She spied Trace on the patio and hurried outside. "I have to leave right away." She wiped a wet spot from her cheek. "Grandfather's worse."

"I'll go with you."

"There's not enough time." She turned to get her purse and fumbled for her keys.

"I'll call the airport and make two emergency reservations for New Mexico."

"I don't have time to quarrel about this. You don't understand. Father isn't an easy person. He won't be cordial toward you. Your—" She stopped her words and glanced at the floor.

His voice rose. "I'm part Indian."

"I'm sorry." She moved closer and touched his arm. "Father can be prejudiced."

"Are you ashamed of me?"

She stared at Trace, wary of the conversation. There wasn't time for this discussion. Still, the situation could define the rest of their relationship.

"Trace, you've never embarrassed me. I'm proud to be in your company."

"Are you sure?"

"I've never been more positive."

"Good, you go back to Bellmore and pack. Leave the travel plans to me. I'll text you when I've secured a flight and pick you up. Don't worry about your Father. I can handle myself. Allow me to speak with your grandfather. This is important to him."

"You're right, let's hurry."

"Go." He led her to the car. "I'll contact you shortly."

Barbary sped down the country road to get back to her room. She jogged inside and informed the desk she needed to leave immediately and gave her credit card to the receptionist. Seconds later, she rushed to the suite and recklessly tossed her clothes inside the luggage. Her phone beeped with a text—*Seats held. We leave n hour, pick u up 15 n lobby.*

She typed "*k*" and secured her belongings for the flight.

Barbary stood in the lobby of the inn. Trace grabbed her luggage. "Let's go. We'll have to hurry to catch the flight."

"Wait! Trace, I have a rental car to deal with."

"No, one of my men will handle the return. Leave your keys at the desk."

Barbary followed Trace to his truck and glanced out the window at the huge pine trees, un-sure of what to expect when she returned home.

She reached across the seat and touched his Trace's hand. "Thank you. No one's stood by me the way you're doing."

"I'll endure any hardship for you." He turned into the airport.

"You mean you'll be longsuffering."

Before Barbary stepped inside the terminal, she lightly kissed him. "I hope meeting Father doesn't end the good beginning we have."

Seventeen

The pilot announced they were landing, and Barbary glanced from the window toward the man she loved. They deplaned and stepped into the New Mexico airport, and went to baggage claim. Trace gathered the luggage, while Barbary tapped her screen and called the driver.

"Hector, I'm at the terminal, please come get us."

"Certainly." The driver paused. "I'm sorry. Did you say us?"

"Yes, I did." She glanced at Trace. "Someone special is with me."

"Very well."

"Hector. ask Mia to prepare the guest suite."

"Yes, ma'am."

Barbary and Trace stood outside at the curb. She looked ahead, watching for the driver. "You'll like Mia. To me, she's part of the family, even though Father gets irritated with her. After Mother passed away, I don't know what I'd have done without her. She tucked me into bed many nights."

"Mia sounds like a good person."

"There's Hector." She moved back when the driver pulled close to the sidewalk and got out to load the luggage.

"Hector, this is Trace."

"Nice to meet you, sir." The driver shook Trace's hand.

"Please, call me Trace." He held the door for Barbary and took his seat. "I've never been to New Mexico. Always wanted to travel more, seems I stay too busy with work."

"I'm glad you joined me, but Father will be a challenge."

"I've put up with people who share your father's notions. I'll be fine." He leaned close and kissed her cheek.

"Hector, pull into the lower driveway. We'll enter by way of the kitchen. I want Trace to meet Mia before Father gives him the third degree."

"Of course, Ms. Barbary. I hope you don't mind me saying, your father is short-minded where people's nationalities are concerned."

"Poor Mia is still mad at him for the way he acted when her sister from Mexico City came to visit."

The driver turned into the driveway of the Willis residence.

"Hector, please take our things upstairs."

"Certainly, Ms. Barbary."

Barbary hurried from the car with Trace by her side. "I'll introduce you to Mia. While you two talk, I'll tell father we have company."

"Barbary, I understand you need to tell your father about me first."

"Father knows a little about you. He saw the selfie I took of us on the golf cart."

She noticed the cook coming from the pantry. "Mia, meet Trace."

"So, this is the young man who stole your heart?" Mia shook his hand with a wide grin.

"I stole her heart, huh?" Trace glanced from Mia to Barbary. "Music to my ears, beautiful lady."

"Don't go getting a big head Show Trace the guest suite. I need to speak with Father."

Barbary looked at Trace. "I'll come up in a few minutes and introduce you to Grandfather."

~ * ~

Father stared out the window. Barbary quietly walked up to him. "How is Grandfather?"

"Weak," Father's usual bitter tone now sympathetic. "The doctor says all we can do is to make him comfortable. His heart is giving out. He's so much like your mother."

"Yes, Mother was a carbon copy of Grandfather." Barbary glanced at her father. The softer side of his attitude stayed hidden for so long, she had forgotten he could have an understanding heart. "Grandfather realizes his sickness is taking over. You know what he wishes?"

"What?"

"He wants to make sure he goes to heaven." Father abruptly turned and stared at her. Barbary stepped back a few feet. Time clicked by. When he offered no response, she added, "For Mother, and many people, Heaven is a promise they cling to."

"I suppose you're right. I never discouraged your mother from her faith."

"My job interview took place in Asheville, North Carolina." She bit her cheek at the disapproval in his eyes. "I didn't plan any of this. I created an account with an online employment agency and uploaded my resume. Bellmore invited me to interview."

"I see." He faced the window once more. "Grandfather will be pleased. I suppose I should get used to my family leaving."

Barbary eyed the back of his pristine white shirt. His posture drooped. For the first time in years, she wanted to comfort him. "You'll never lose me. I'm your daughter." She moved closer and hugged him. "Grandfather says the reason we quarrel is because we're both strong-willed."

"He does? If you move, this house will be too silent."

"If I should get the position in North Carolina, I will come back once a month to see you, and to give you grief." She grinned.

"I would like that." He gently hugged her. "You better go see Grandfather. He's asking for you."

"I will." She paused. "I brought Trace with me. He's the man in the photo you saw. He's in the guest room. He came to speak with Grandfather about Heaven."

"You have him here, in this house?"

Barbary watched her father's face twist with fury. Like Hyde to Jekyll, his appearance chilled the room. "For your information, Trace is a respected man and a wonderful person. He's also special to me, so I'll ask you to be civil. Grandfather wants to see him, consider this one of his last wishes."

Eighteen

Barbary knocked on her grandfather's door.

"Come in." His response barely a whisper.

She plastered on her best grin and entered. "I hear you're not feeling well today."

"I'm… having trouble breathing." His clipped words came slow. "I'm afraid my days of listening to my books are over. I wish I held the assurance your beautiful mother did the day she left us."

"I love you, Grandfather." She pulled a chair close and swallowed a lump that burned her throat. "I brought someone to visit you. He's a Christian, like Mother."

"Your young man from Asheville?"

"He wants to talk with you."

"Let the young man come. If your father raises the roof, tell him I requested to see him."

"Don't worry. I've spoken to Father."

"Good."

"I'll see if he's settled and bring him to visit." She rose and exited the room.

Barbary leaned against the wall, squeezed her eyes shut and swiped the tears from her lashes before she lightly tapped on Trace's door.

He greeted her and wrapped his arms around her.

She laid her head on his chest and let the sadness flow. Minutes later, Barbary moved back and touched a button on his shirt. "I'm sorry. I've gotten you wet."

"Honey, don't stress. You can cry on my shoulder anytime." He softly kissed her forehead. "How is your grandfather?"

"Not good. He wants to see you."

"Okay. I brought my Bible in case your grandfather wants to learn more about our Savior."

"Thanks."

Trace walked to the door. "Shall we go?"

"Yes, and I spoke to Father, don't expect him to be nice. He's a hard man."

"I'm here for you and your grandfather. Anything else will be handled with kid gloves."

"I don't understand."

"Your father is battling sorrow of his own. Sad situations often make people act foolish."

Barbary took Trace's hand and walked beside him down the hall. "Grandfather?"

"Come," his voice sounded raspy.

She stepped into his room with Trace. "This is Trace Youngbird."

"What a unique family name." Grandfather held out a feeble hand.

"Nice to meet you, sir. Barbary speaks wonderful things about you."

Grandfather grinned. "I like this fellow. Sit for a spell." He pointed to the chair.

Barbary moved a chair closer. "Here. I'll relax in the window seat."

"Barbary tells me you spent time in Asheville at Bellmore house when you were younger."

"Indeed. I always wanted to go back one day. Tell me about your fascinating heritage."

"I'm part Eastern Cherokee, on my father's side. My mother is pale, like you." He grinned when Grandfather chuckled. "Mom taught me about Jesus, and the sacrifice He made for everyone who repents and accepts Him in their hearts."

Barbary watched the exchange between the men and mulled over the moment that was sure to become embedded in her heart forever. Two important people in her life were enjoying each other's company.

She eyed Grandfather and compared him to Father. Her love for Father strong, but Grandfather represented the last link to her mother. Barbary discreetly wiped moisture from her eyes and turned her attention back to the men.

Grandfather leaned his head into the pillow. "Before my daughter died she read the Bible and talked about the Lord." He took a breath. "I want to understand how I can go to Heaven."

Trace opened his Bible. "First let me read John 3:16." His voice filled the room as he described Jesus' walk on earth, and quoted passages.

"Son, I do want to be in good standing with Christ. I'm one of those sinners the Bible speaks of."

"In Romans 10:9-10 God's word says, 'If you declare with your mouth, Jesus is Lord, and believe in your heart, God raised Him from the dead, you will be saved...'" Trace continued to read.

Grandfather closed his eyes. Time crawled before he looked at Trace. "I accept Jesus as Lord. Now, I understand why my daughter loved Him."

Barbary smiled. From listening she also discovered what being a Christian meant.

Trace reached for Grandfather's hand. "If you'll repeat a few words after me, you can be saved."

"I want to."

"We'll go slow." Trace closed his eyes. "Father, I ask you to forgive me of my sins..." He waited for Grandfather to utter the words, Barbary listened and silently repeated the phrase.

Trace continued the sinner's prayer, paused, and listened to Grandfather's exhausted tone repeat the words.

"Thank You, Lord, for hearing my prayer, and saving me according to Your word. In Jesus name, Amen."

When Grandfather finished, Trace rose from his seat and hugged the older man. "You're now part of the family of God. When you leave this world, you'll be in Heaven."

Grandfather strained to speak. "Hot-dog, Barbary. Thank you for Trace."

"You're welcome." She rose from her seat and kissed his cheek. "Rest."

They stepped into the hallway. "Trace, I appreciate what you did."

"I only introduced him to the Lord."

Barbary hugged him. "You did a lot."

~ * ~

Barbary walked with Trace to the dining room for dinner. She waited for him to pull the chair out for her, the way he usually did, then he took the seat beside her.

"Mia, where's Father?"

"He's in the library with Regina. She brought some paperwork by for him to sign." Mia placed a roast on the table along with a couple of side dishes.

"Thank you." Barbary waited for Trace to say the blessing. Afterwards, she repeated, "Amen."

"This is wonderful. Mia cooks a roast the correct way, not like mine." He pointed to the platter.

Barbary laughed. "You tried."

They finished dinner. Barbary rose from her seat. "Would you like to see the garden?"

"Of course." He held out his arm for Barbary to take.

"This is a small flower patch compared to what you're used to." Barbary pointed to the ground. "My favorite is the Mexican Feather Grass."

Trace bent down and touched the tiny purple, feathery blooms. "Also called, Russian Sage."

"I should realize by now, you know all the flowers by name."

After another look at the flowers, they walked the grounds, stopping every so often to cuddle. Barbary yawned. "We had a long day, and I should go inside."

"All the way from North Carolina to New Mexico. I have to admit, I'm tired, too." He led her back to the house.

Barbary stood in front of the door of the guest room. "I'm happy you're here."

"I needed to come."

"I'm going to check on Grandfather before I turn in."

"I'll see you in the morning." He gave her a quick caress, turned and shut the door.

Barbary strolled to the end of the hall and knocked on the door. She put her ear close to her his response.

"Yes."

"Grandfather, I wanted to say goodnight." She kissed his cheek.

"Trace is a good man. Don't let anyone tell you otherwise. I'd be proud to have him in the family." He took a ragged breath.

"He is special. I'm going to let you rest."

"Love you, always." The syllables broke from his forced words.

"I love you, too."

She left his room and went down the hall to her room. With a heavy heart Barbary slipped under the covers. In her mind she replayed Trace and Grandfather's visit, while the events of the day slowly faded into dreams.

~ * ~

Trace sat on the side of the bed. For hours, sleep escaped him. Mia's leftover roast seemed to call. He grabbed his robe and went down the stairs.

He ascended the bottom step and came face to face with Barbary's father. "Sir, I don't think we've met. I'm Trace." He ignored the once over Barbary's father gave him and put his hand out in greeting.

"Humph." His nostrils flared. "I know who you are. I never thought someone of your caliber would entice my daughter."

Trace silently asked the Lord for guidance. "Sir, I would never sway your daughter to do anything she didn't want to do. In case you haven't noticed, she is a grown woman. Furthermore, your opinions are of no value."

"No value?" He leaned back on his heels. "I'm not surprised you don't care."

"I do care, and my importance is placed on God, and living a contented life. I came with Barbary to ease her grandfather's mind about salvation. I pray for the day you let go of the bitterness eating at you." He turned and made his way back upstairs.

Nineteen

Barbary opened her eyes from a deep sleep. Unexplained sadness gripped her, chill bumps covered her arms, along with a sense of dread. She jumped from the bed and slipped into her robe.

When she got to the hallway, Trace and Mia were at the bottom of the stairs, whispering. Her father stood at the door with a man in an EMS uniform.

"No!" She rushed down the steps.

"Barbary honey, please stop." Trace met her at the bottom step.

Barbary eyed him. "Grandfather?"

"Yes." He hugged her. "He's gone to Heaven."

Barbary buried her head in his chest and wept. "Why?"

"Barbary." Father closed the distance between them.

Trace whispered. "Your father needs you."

She moved away from Trace and put her arms around her father. "When?"

"Earlier this morning."

"Grandfather wanted to be with Mother in Heaven. Trace gave him that assurance." She glanced at her father and toward the man she loved.

Father looked sideways at Trace. "I'm not a man who likes to be wrong. Still, I recognize the way you look at my daughter. I've seen the same look in her eyes. She cares for you. You coming here made Grandfather happy. There are some things I can't change and must accept."

~ * ~

Summer turned to fall. Barbary put the final touches on an advertisement highlighting the coming holiday attraction at Bellmore. She locked her office door and rushed to her suite.

In her room, she picked up a framed picture of Grandfather. "I wish you were here. Our lives are so different with Trace around. He asked me to be his *ah-chee-ye-hi*. It means, wife in Cherokee. Can you believe Father and Regina are dating too?" She placed the picture back on the table.

~ * ~

The next day the vibrant sun highlighted the autumn colors of the trees. Barbary stood in one corner of the conservatory at Bellmore gardens. She couldn't think of a better place to have a wedding than where she met her fiancé.

The music changed, Father joined her and took her hand. "Are you ready?" He whispered.

"Very much." She kissed her father's cheek. "I love you."

"And I you, my dear." Together they took measured steps down the aisle.

Barbary eyed the way Trace's dark hair shined against the pale gray tuxedo. Her cheeks hurt from grinning so much. Still, she couldn't stop the joy.

She held her father's arm and nodded at Regina while she moved toward Trace and the Minister.

"Who presents this woman to be married to this man?"

"I do." Father kissed Barbary's cheek and joined Regina.

Barbary took her place beside Trace as the ceremony began.

She focused on the vows. "To love and cherish forever."

Her smile widened even more to welcome the words that represented the foundation of her new life.

Barbary tilted her head and looked into the loving eyes of her husband, silently attempting to convey all of the things his love meant to her. *Barbary Youngbird. Perfect.*

~ *End* ~

Mary L. Ball is a multi-published Christian author and resides in the heart of North Carolina. When she isn't working on her latest story, she enjoys fishing, reading, and ministering in song with her husband.

Readers can connect with her on her web page, Facebook or Twitter.

http://www.marylball.com
https://www.facebook.com/gracefulbooks/
https://twitter.com/inspires4mary

55876354R00083

Made in the USA
Columbia, SC
18 April 2019